Temple Israel Library
Minneapolis, Minn.

———

Please sign your full name on the above card.

Return books promptly to the Library or Temple Office.

Fines will be charged for overdue books or for damage or loss of same.

ALAN
AND
NAOMI

ALAN
AND
NAOMI

by Myron Levoy

HARPER & ROW, PUBLISHERS

Alan and Naomi
Copyright © 1977 by Myron Levoy
For information address Harper & Row, Publishers, Inc., 10 East 53rd Street, New York, N.Y. 10022.

Library of Congress Cataloging in Publication Data
Levoy, Myron.
    Alan and Naomi.

    SUMMARY: In New York of the 1940's a boy tries to befriend a girl traumatized by Nazi brutality in France.
    [1. Friendship—Fiction. 2. New York (City)—Fiction. 3. Mentally ill—Fiction] I. Title.
PZ7.L5825A1   [Fic]   76-41522
ISBN 0-06-023799-6
ISBN 0-06-023800-3 lib. bdg.

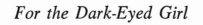

For the Dark-Eyed Girl

1

Alan Silverman took some tight half-swings with the stickball bat, chewing his wad of gum as if it were tobacco. It was growing too dark to see. Alan watched Joe Condello's right hand; Joe had a trick of pitching suddenly, without a windup.

Alan needed a hit; he hadn't been able to connect all afternoon. He took a few more swings, the way DiMaggio did. Then the pitch came down, low and outside.

"Ball! One and one!"

"That was over!" shouted Condello.

"Over the Bronx!" called Shaun Kelly, the captain of Alan's team. "That was so wide you could drive a Mack truck through it."

"How about a decent pitch, Condello, huh?" Alan called, trying to sound like Shaun. But he knew the moment he said it, that he actually sounded like Alan Silverman, with that uncertain huh at the end. That half-apology.

"Cars!" someone called.

Passing cars were an automatic time-out. Alan walked

over to the curb with the others and let his mind float. It was Yankee Stadium. He had just rounded the bases and was jogging to the dugout, while above him the crowd roared. He had done it! The headlines in the *Daily News*, the *Times*, the *Mirror*, the *Post* all screamed: *AL SILVERMAN BREAKS RUTH'S RECORD! SIXTY-FIRST AND SIXTY-SECOND HOME RUNS IN SAME GAME! YANKEE FANS GO WILD! PARADE DOWN BROADWAY PLANNED!*

But the majestic applause in his ears died as the cars passed, and the towering stadium became his apartment building again. The Oak Terrace Arms. Five stories with neither oaks nor terraces, just hallways and heavy metal apartment doors painted brown to look like oak or hickory or moldy chocolate. The Oak Terrace Arms with its old-fashioned chandelier in the lobby. And Finch, the crankiest superintendent in the U.S.A.

The cars were gone. "Play ball!" Joe Condello shouted. "It's getting dark."

Alan stepped up to the plate again, knocking imaginary dirt from his shoes with the stickball bat. He crouched, the bat held way back. Joe wound up, looked toward first, then hesitated.

"Balk!" someone called.

"Like hell! The game's over, that's what!" Joe shouted. "Called account of darkness. We won!"

"What do you mean!" Shaun Kelly walked over. "We didn't get our licks! You can't win if we don't get our licks!"

"That's just tough, Kelly! When it gets dark, the game's

over. That's the rule."

Alan threw the bat to the ground as if he were angry, but inside he was relieved. He hadn't seen that last pitch at all. Joe was being dumb as usual; the darkness was in his favor. But when Joe Condello decided something, that was that.

Alan tried to sound like Shaun again. "Even if you won, so what? We still beat you the last three games in a row."

"But not by five points, Silverman! We won by five points! Eat 'em for dinner. Point, point, point, point, *point*! Eat 'em with your herring."

"Hey!" called Shaun. "Get that, Al! He can count to five! I saw a horse who could do that in Barnum and Bailey. Only thing is, the horse could count to *six*!"

"Shut your freaken mouth, Kelly! You and Silverman! Some pair! You Jew-lover, you!"

Get him for that, Alan thought. Even if you can't beat him. Even if— Don't think! Just get him!

Joe spit on the ground near Alan. Then he turned and walked away, bouncing the ball high with total contempt. As Alan lunged toward Condello, Shaun grabbed Alan's arm and twisted it behind his back and up.

"Let go my arm, Shaun!"

"Shut up," Shaun hissed at him. "Condello can kill you. . . . Hey, Condello! Don't wet your bed! Nighty-night."

"Up yours, freaken Jew-lover!" Joe called, spitting again. Joe kept right on walking. He was heavier than Shaun, but he knew that Shaun Kelly was the fastest, trickiest fighter in the neighborhood. Joe had lost too many fights to him. Lost them before he could use his weight against Shaun, before he could land a solid punch.

Alan struggled to free himself. "I don't need your help, damn it! Let go, Kelly!"

"You don't need my help, bull! You're crazy! Forget about Condello. Who cares about him. Besides, I gotta eat; I don't have time for fights." Shaun released his grip. Condello was gone.

Alan stepped back from Shaun to turn his anger into distance. "Thanks a lot," he said, rubbing his arm above the elbow.

"You're welcome. No charge."

Alan shook his arm and bent it three or four times the way a batter does when he's been hit in the elbow with a bad pitch. Then he picked up the bat and cracked it angrily on the sidewalk.

"Good shot," said Shaun. "You'll break the bat."

They walked silently toward the lobby of the Oak Terrace Arms. Alan pushed the big iron-grilled lobby door, walking ahead of Shaun. The door's hinges screeched a tune as it opened, and a slower, sadder one as it closed behind them. It sounded like a baby crying, or an angry cat, or a long-tailed demon.

Shaun lived on the second floor; Alan's apartment was on the third. Sometimes they stopped to talk for a minute outside Shaun's door before Alan went up the next flight. They paused in the hallway and shuffled.

"See you in the morning, I guess," said Alan, sullenly. They always walked to junior high together. Alan clicked the stickball bat against the tiled floor of the hallway. There was a slight echo. He clicked faster, trying to overtake the echo.

"Joe Condello can turn you into mashed potatoes," said Shaun. Alan kept clicking the bat. "You're not too smart, you know. Maybe you're good with school stuff, but you don't know when to lay off. . . . So you're Jewish, so what? I'm Catholic. So you're a Catholic-lover, so what? Who cares?"

Alan whispered in the echoing hallway, "Your father cares. He doesn't want me to hang around with you."

"Neither does yours," Shaun whispered back.

"*He* doesn't care. . . . Maybe my mother does, a little. . . . I don't know." Alan kept tapping the stickball bat, not looking up.

"So what? They don't own us. I do what I want. How about you?"

"I do what I want, too. . . ." Alan wondered if he really did.

"OK," said Shaun, as if that solved it.

"OK."

"Good night, Jew."

"Good night, Catholic."

"Screwball."

"Jerk."

"G'night." Alan turned and raced up the next flight. Maybe they really *were* friends. They'd never talked about it before. The Jewish-Catholic stuff. It felt good. It made Alan want to take three steps at a time.

He reached his landing and stopped short; there was a

girl kneeling near his door, blocking his way. She was tearing a piece of paper into little scraps. It was the new girl in the building, that crazy girl from upstairs. He had seen her rush through the lobby yesterday with her mother.

Her eyes were so big, so round with fear that her thin face seemed to be all eyes. Like in the movies. The horror films. The fear of the next slightest sound.

Only her hands moved, busily tearing the sheet of paper, forming little white flakes all around her, on her dress, on the tiles.

Alan remembered how his father had spoken to a puppy once, starving and frightened in front of the house. The puppy had had the same eyes.

"Hello . . . hello . . ." Alan said. He took a small step forward, then another. The girl stood up, pressing against the wall. The bits of paper on her dress fell like snow to the floor.

"I'm going to my door," Alan said softly, almost in a whisper. "OK? . . . I live here. . . . OK?"

The girl moved, with her back against the wall, to the farthest corner. *"Non! Non!"* she suddenly called, dropping the sheet of paper she'd been tearing.

Alan remembered his father saying the girl was a war refugee from France; she and her mother were living with the Liebmans upstairs. Second cousins, or something.

The girl called again, *"Non! Non! Laissez-moi tranquille!"* She was staring at the stickball bat.

Alan understood only the "No! No!," but he decided it was the stickball bat that was frightening her. He laid the sawed-off broomstick on the tiled floor, then rolled it toward his door. The bat whirred along the tiles.

The girl kept staring at the bat as if it were a python poised to strike.

She's crazy all right, Alan thought. The guys are right. She's really crazy. But . . . maybe she'll listen to me in French.

Alan had just started taking French, and he knew only a few phrases, like "hello" and "good-bye" and "What's your name?" and "How are you?"

"Uh . . . *Bonjour.* . . . *Comment allez-vous?* . . . Huh? . . . You know, *comment allez-vous?*"

The girl looked wildly from side to side for an escape path. Alan stepped out of the way, and as he did, the girl sprang past him and up the flight of stairs to the floor above.

What had he done? What was wrong with saying "Hello, how are you?" Alan waited a moment, listening. It was absolutely still in the hallway; no door opened or closed on the next floor. She must be waiting in her hallway, too; waiting and listening.

Alan walked over, very quietly, and picked up the piece of torn paper. It was part of a map, a map of New York City. On it were some meaningless lines in red pencil, and a few words in a shaky hand, which read: GEHEIME STAATSPOLIZEI. Alan hesitated, then stuffed the paper in his pocket.

He went to his door and picked up the stickball bat. It made a slight clatter on the tiles. And instantly, he heard a high wailing voice from the hallway above: *"Maman!*

Maman! Ils sont en bas! Ils sont en bas! Maman! Mamaaan!"

Alan felt he'd heard that voice somewhere before. Its sharp-edged terror cut loose all the shadows, filling the hallway with demons, like the metallic screech of the lobby door.

2

It was good to get inside, away from that cry, to the smell of chicken with dumplings simmering in the big pot. His mother called to him from the kitchen, and her scolding voice was safe and comfortable, like the moist smells of the food.

"Alan! Why are you late again? Your father is home! You didn't even see him come in downstairs, with your baseball game. You don't even notice your own fa—"

"Stickball!"

"Stickball? On your head is where the stick belongs, yes? Wash up!" Her face appeared at the kitchen door, large, and round, and sagging at the mouth a little. "Your father is upset. The war. Who knows. So be as quiet as a mouse. . . . Why are you so flushed?"

Alan went into the living room. His father was studying a large map of Europe glued to thick cardboard. The map was prickly with pins representing the fighting fronts.

"Alan . . ." his father began. He looked at Alan and shook his head slowly. Then he started rearranging some of the pins.

"Things are bad, huh?" asked Alan. It was the war, all right.

"What can I tell you. It looked so easy. It looked *too* easy. Eisenhower isn't thinking. He advanced too fast. Now the German line is holding."

"I'm sorry."

"You're sorry? It's not your fault. It's too much over-confidence they have, that's all."

"I mean, I'm sorry I'm late for dinner. It was just that we were in the middle of a stickball game and—"

"Supper? Who can worry about that. Your mother is upset, maybe, because it's her best dish. Me? I'd eat bread and water if we could only win this war already. . . . Alan, play your games. Thank God, you're free to play your games and forget supper. Thank God, I say."

They had dinner in the kitchen. Alan's mother always said it was too much fuss for just the three of them to eat at the dining-room table. When they had company, that was different. Besides, Alan's mother felt the kitchen table was better, warmer, nearer to the stove, and in her own mother's house had always been the center of family activity. The kitchen was home.

But tonight, his mother's thoughts seemed far away from cooking and dinner. She scarcely ate. As she cleared away the dishes, she said, "Now I want to talk." She always said that, in just that way, when there was something serious to discuss.

"What is it, Ruth, what?" asked Alan's father. "The superintendent again? Finch?"

"No, no. Not Finch. . . . You have your coffee, Sol;

you have your milk, Alan; and I'll talk. There's marble cake, day-old, but good."

Alan sighed. Why did his mother always have to make big dramas out of everything? Why couldn't she just say whatever she wanted to say?

"Listen. You too, Alan. Listen. But let me finish, to the end!"

"You haven't said anything," Sol complained. "If you begin, then maybe we can let you finish."

"All right. You know Mrs. Kirshenbaum and her daughter, Naomi, yes? Living with the Liebmans?"

Alan knew. It was the crazy girl.

"Well let me tell you, they went through plenty getting out of France. All kinds of things. They had to hide in the bottom of a sewer for four days without food. Forever hiding, forever running. Somehow, they got over the border to Switzerland. And then, it still took three years for the Liebmans to finally get them over here—"

"This we know," Alan's father interrupted.

"I *don't* know," said Alan. "What's wrong with her? I saw her out in the hallway before, and she looks really crazy. She even sounds crazy."

"She's *not* crazy!" his mother said, sharply. "And don't you ever let me hear you call her that—"

"All right, so go on, already," said Sol.

"Then listen. I heard more today from Mrs. Liebman. That child has been through everything. *Everything!* Her father was killed by the Nazis, you know that. But listen. They beat him to death, right in front of that girl's eyes. She was only eight years old then. Those animals! . . .

When the mother comes home from a neighbor, whatever, he's lying there covered with blood. And the girl is next to him, trying to wipe off the blood, as if that could make him alive again. She was covered head to foot in her own father's blood, that little child—"

"All right, Ruth. We know what kind of things they've done."

Alan tried to picture it in his mind, but he couldn't. Everything seemed to be in black and white, like some of the war movies he'd seen. Even the blood was gray.

"Her husband had joined the French Resistance. A Jew. That's all they needed. They found him; they killed him. That's it. But the girl, Naomi . . . she's never been the same. Not crazy! Just . . . not the same. Four years ago, it happened. It's very hard for the mother. Sometimes the girl is better, sometimes worse."

"Mom, she looked—you don't want me to say it, but she looked insane to me."

"She needs help. A lot of help. I think they're making a mistake. They bring this girl here, to a mixed neighborhood, not such a good neighborhood—I'm sorry, Sol, but it isn't a very good—"

Sol put down his coffee. "Who said it was? What does the City of New York pay? We can't afford better. I'm sorry I'm not Mayor LaGuardia; I'm just in the Department of Records."

Alan had always been awed by the fact that his father worked with birth certificates, and marriage and death certificates, but his mother often complained that it wasn't really a good job.

"Sol, I'm not blaming you. It's just that they *have* to live with the Liebmans. They have no money, nothing. They're stuck here. This is it for them."

"*And* for us!" Sol said, crankily.

"Sol, please, no fights. . . . Anyway, the girl needs friends. Children her age. Nice children. A few. One! And who is there? The Liebmans have a son in the Army, some good that is. There's no one her age. Not even close. Before she can go to school again, the doctor says she has to learn to—to play. To trust. That's the word: to trust."

Alan felt a net, a huge fishing net, closing around him. He knew he'd better slip out fast. "Not me," he said. "She's a girl; and she's crazy; and I *won't!*"

"Alan, have I asked you?"

"*Yes!*"

"Let your mother talk, Alan," said his father. "Let her finish."

"All right, Alan. I know your baseball is very important—"

"STICKBALL!"

"But there are other things in the world—"

"Why *me*?"

"There's no one else."

"No!"

"All you have to do, you go upstairs once a day, after school, an hour, a half hour, you go upstairs and you just sit. Quietly. Maybe you take a—"

"No! I won't! I can't!"

"A toy, who knows . . . you have all kinds of things. Like a little airplane, a car . . . We have all your old

19

cars, the little ones—"

"That's for babies! No!"

"Alan, it isn't for me I'm asking—"

"I won't do it. I have enough problems the way it is. Some of the guys call me sissy sometimes! The only thing I can do is play stickball! It's the only thing I'm good at. The only thing! I got one friend on the block, that's all. And he'll quit on me! She's a girl! And she's crazy!"

"There's the Hebrew School boys—"

"That's a mile away! I can't be friends a mile away!"

"Sol, talk to him. I give up."

"Dad, I can't! It's not fair! Don't make me do this. *Please!*"

His father was thinking. Alan began to have hopes. His father was thinking, not answering quickly, and that was good. Maybe his father understood.

"Alan," his father said, "we can't make you do this, no. You're right. It isn't fair. And besides, this is very delicate. Like a surgical operation. Who would use a surgeon who hates what he's doing? He could cut off your nose, your ears, even your whole head. Zzzt! Like that. Gone. . . . No, we can't force you. But—allow me one but. In our life, Alan, sometimes when we're young, sometimes when we're old, in our life, once or twice, we're called upon to do something we can't do, that we don't want to do, that we won't do. But we do it."

"Well *I* won't!"

"We'll see. . . . Why do we do it? It's a mystery. Maybe to prove that what we *are* is something a little more than what we think we are. You've asked me, Alan,

I remember, you've asked more than once: how could God allow the things the Nazis are doing. The things Hitler is doing. Where is God, you asked me. Those were the hardest questions of my life. It isn't easy; it isn't simple. It's like asking why do people die. And you said you didn't believe in God. I remember telling you that possibly, someday, a very surprising thing might happen. God would find *you*. When you least expected it. Could that be what this is all about? I'm an old-fashioned man. I believe it. So we'll see. I want you to think about it very hard tonight. But I want you to know this: I won't force you to do anything you can't do. Just think about it. All right?"

"Why *me*?"

"Maybe, because you're lucky."

"Enough philosophy," said Alan's mother. "I have to tell Mrs. Liebman *something*."

"Tell her that we'll have an answer in a day. It's a big question. It takes a little time."

"All right, Sol. But I hope you know what you're doing with all your philosophy all the time."

"If I knew what I was doing, I'd not only be Mayor LaGuardia, I'd be President Roosevelt. But then again, Roosevelt has a very smart wife. She suggests this or that to the President. She doesn't put a gun to his head."

"Enough, Sol."

"Think about it, Alan. That's all I ask. Will you?"

"I . . . I guess so. . . ."

"That's all I ask."

3

Alan lay on his bed, his mathematics book face down on his stomach. Math! Jane's age and Tom's age and this car going twice as fast as that car. Why couldn't they make it interesting? Why couldn't they have something about baseball averages or a Spitfire going twice as fast as a Messerschmitt? Alan looked at his model of a Supermarine Spitfire suspended from the ceiling by a length of kite string. It was turning very slowly, high above his desk. He had learned to draw its thin sleek profile in math class, and every other page of his notebook had Spitfires roaring down the margin in wrenching dives. Sometimes he wondered if it was unpatriotic to like a British plane better than any American plane, including the P-40 with its angry shark's mouth painted on the underbelly. But the P-40 *was* a close second.

How could any girl, anywhere, ever understand anything about pursuit planes? Especially a crazy girl. Shaun Kelly and he fought endlessly on the way to school over the merits of the P-40 versus the Spitfire. And the Yanks versus the Brooklyn Dodgers. They talked about stickball and about flying their model planes. They told each other the latest dirty jokes circulating round the class. What would a girl talk about? She couldn't speak English, anyway. It was dumb. It was just plain dumb.

His mother could play with that girl herself. Let *her* try it for a while.

"Because you're lucky," his father had said. Lucky? Lucky for what? Probably, to be alive. His father had said that many times. Lucky to be alive in America. That *was* luck all right. If he'd been born in Germany or Poland or France, he'd probably be in a concentration camp now. Or he'd be hiding somewhere. Running from the Nazis. He'd probably be . . .

He didn't let himself finish the thought. He took up the math book and stared at the next problem. Another age problem. Who cares how old anyone is! Who cares if Jack is a million times older than Mack.

Then the thought slipped out. He'd probably be like Naomi. Crouching in the hallway. Afraid of a stickball bat.

Alan remembered the map she'd been tearing. He sat up and took the scrap of paper from his pocket. He decided to examine it, the way Ellery Queen would, for clues.

Could those red lines mean anything? Some had arrows attached to them. They reminded him of a battle map, like his father's map of the war fronts. And those words: GEHEIME STAATSPOLIZEI. They sounded German, not French. Maybe the girl and her mother were actually spies. Alan let a headline flash in his mind: *AL SILVER-MAN, PRIVATE EYE, DISCOVERS NEW YORK HIDEOUT OF NAZI SPIES FROM MYSTERY MAP*

Yes, spies. And the words were a code. The lines, a secret route.

GEHEIME STAATSPOLIZEI. Maybe every odd letter. GHIETASO . . . No. Every even letter. EEMSATP . . . No. Then what? STAATS sounded like States. POLIZEI. Polish? Polish States? Maybe. GEHEIME. Go home? Go home Polish States? . . . No. . . . Police? State Police? That must be it. GEHEIME . . .

Then suddenly Alan saw. *Geheime Staatspolizei*. Ge-Sta-Po. GESTAPO! The Nazi Secret Police! The Gestapo! They *were* spies! She and her mother!

No . . . no? . . . That wasn't it at all. That wasn't it. But for a flickering second he wished it were true, wished the map had secret instructions to blow up New York. But no, of course they weren't spies; they were victims. The words on the map had been written by the girl in fear. From something crazy in her mind.

That face. Had it ever smiled? He tried to picture Naomi laughing, but he couldn't. Did she sit huddled in a corner of her room tearing up maps all night? Did she ever listen to the radio, or read a book? Did she ever sing, or say something funny, or talk to anyone? You might just as well be dead.

Alan went to his window and looked at the apartments across the courtyard. He knew every window from years of living in the same building. The Liebmans had the two

24

windows above, on the left. One window was lit; the other was dark. And at the dark window, he saw the girl staring out.

Alan knew it was a bedroom window. All the bedroom windows lined up, one above the other, and all the living-room windows, too.

Alan waved to the girl, but she didn't move. Had she seen him? Yes, he was sure she had. She was looking right at him. He waved again. Why didn't she wave back? What could she be afraid of now? There was a courtyard between them.

Maybe she was thinking about her father; her father all covered with blood. Alan tried to picture his own father lying on the floor, bleeding and dying, but he couldn't. He just couldn't. In his thoughts, his father stirred, and made a funny face, only playing at being wounded, trying to make Alan laugh.

If only I could make Naomi laugh, right now, he thought.

Alan glanced around his bedroom quickly. What could he show her that was funny? His model airplane? The Spitfire? It wasn't funny; it might even scare her. No war stuff. . . . His magician's hat and mustache? That could be funny. But still . . . it might scare her, too.

Alan opened his closet door and searched through the wreckage of old toys. A homemade sailboat. Not funny. A Tinkertoy set. Not for this. Fielder's glove, plaster-of-paris statue kit, dump truck, broken ukelele. No, they weren't any good. Then he saw his old, beat-up Charlie McCarthy dummy in the debris. You could make it talk,

25

just like Edgar Bergen did, by pulling a string at the back that moved the lower jaw up and down. Only the jaw wouldn't open anymore, and the head was half off. Still, this might be good.

Alan took the dummy to the window, keeping it below the sill. Naomi was still looking out, toward his window. He raised the dummy slowly and waved its arm toward Naomi. He paused, then waved again.

Naomi abruptly left the window. Alan sighed, then made Charlie McCarthy speak, the way he had years ago, when he'd gotten the toy for his eighth birthday.

"I guess our show's a flop, Mr. Bergen," said the dummy.

"Well, Charlie, we all have to have our losers," said Alan.

"That's all right, Mr. Bergen. I'll take you anytime. I'm bighearted that way."

"Behave, Charlie, or I'll put you back in the closet—"

Alan stopped in the middle of his line. Above, across the courtyard, Naomi had reappeared at her window holding a doll. And she was waving the doll's arm.

Alan raised Charlie McCarthy up high and waved his arm furiously. The doll waved back once more, before Naomi disappeared with it into the dark room.

Alan stood and waited, but she didn't return.

"How was that, Mr. Bergen?" Alan made the dummy ask.

"I don't know," said Alan, forgetting to sound like Edgar Bergen. "I guess it was OK."

"OK? It was terrific! She waved back. It was like she

was saying hello," Alan said for the dummy.

"I know," said Alan.

"So what's the problem?" asked McCarthy.

"You *know* what's the problem! Now we're stuck with her, that's what! Now we're gonna *have* to play with her."

"Why?" asked the dummy. "I hate kids. I only like Dorothy Lamour and Lana Turner and all those pinup girls. Ha-cha-cha. You know *me*. I'm Charlie McCarthy. Let's drop her cold, Mr. Bergen."

"We can't."

"Why not?"

"Because she needs us. Right? Right? You know she needs us."

"Anything you say, Mr. Bergen."

"I say she needs us."

"I say you're a sap."

"Shut up!"

"OK, Bergen. You're the boss."

4

Alan shifted his heavy load of books to the other arm as he walked to school with Shaun. Shaun was telling Alan about his new plan for the afternoon stickball game, a plan he called the Kelly Shift. It involved moving an outfielder much farther in, to get the blooper shots that had scored most of the runs in the game last evening. But Alan wasn't really listening.

He was troubled by the way his mother and father had reacted at breakfast.

"Has the jury reached a verdict?" his father had asked.

"Yes," Alan had answered.

"And?"

"And . . . I guess I'll have to do it."

"Does that mean yes, please tell me?" asked his mother. "Or does it mean maybe?"

"It means yes."

They had both looked at him without a word, but he saw his mother's eyes sparkle with tears. And behind him, his father squeezed Alan's shoulder and walked out of the kitchen. The loud blowing of a nose in the living room confirmed Alan's suspicion that his father was in tears, too.

His father didn't cry for nothing, Alan realized. He'd only known it to happen twice before. Once, many years ago, when Alan's baby sister had died in the hospital, three days old. And once, in a movie, when a newsreel had shown Polish Jews, wearing armbands, being pushed into trucks by Nazi soldiers.

It worried Alan. If this was so important, what if he failed? What if he said the wrong thing, or maybe got angry and called the girl a name? What if he made her crazier? What would his parents say then?

"Hey, Al, aren't you listening?" said Shaun.

"Huh?" said Alan, dazed.

"For crying out loud, what do you think of the plan?"

"The plan?"

"The Kelly Shift."

"Oh. . . . It's good. Very good. . . . Uh, say Shaun. I forgot to tell you. I can't play this afternoon. I've got . . . sort of an errand to do." Could he tell Shaun about Naomi, he wondered.

"Then who's gonna catch all the pop shots?" asked Shaun.

"I don't know . . . Tony! He's good! He's very fast."

"What's the errand? Can't you do it after the game? Like around seven?"

"No. It's . . . I promised to do it at four."

"Why?"

"I've got to do homework after."

"You and your homework. Why don't you skip home-

29

work sometimes, like me? If I don't feel like doing it, I don't do it."

"My parents want me to."

"I thought you do what *you* want."

"Well . . . maybe I want to do my homework." Alan knew he had to do his work; it was unquestioned in his home. Skipping homework would be like cutting school, or stealing something in the candy store.

"You're grade-happy," said Shaun. "You're just out to get grades. You want to be first, that's all. That's one of the worst things about you."

"I just have to do my homework; I can't help it. I don't care if I'm first in the class or not. . . . What else is the worst things about me?"

"That's it."

"You said *one* of the worst."

"Well, some of the guys think you're yellow. I don't. But *they* do."

"You wouldn't let me fight yesterday, and now you're calling me—"

"Not me!" Shaun interrupted. "Some of the guys—"

"Who?"

"Never mind. . . . You can probably *guess* who. And who gives a damn what *they* think, right?"

"What else?"

"What else, what?"

"Is no good about me?"

"Nothing else."

"I study too hard, and some guys think I'm yellow?"

"You've got it."

"That's not so bad. I *do* study hard, and I don't care what they think about that. And I *know* I'm not yellow." Alan said it as strongly as possible to convince Shaun, but he hadn't quite convinced himself. He was afraid of Joe Condello, and Fred Kleinholtz, and two or three others. Plenty of others. But yellow didn't mean afraid exactly; it meant you wouldn't fight. And he *would*! . . . Or had he been relieved yesterday when Shaun had grabbed his arm? . . . No! . . . Well, maybe a little . . .

"OK, what's wrong with *me*?" asked Shaun. "Tit for tat, right?"

"Nothing."

"Oh, cut the bull. I want to know."

"Well . . . You're smart, very smart, but you *don't* study. How's that?"

"Great! 'Cause I plan to be an elephant trainer."

"Airline pilots have to have a college degree."

"Who says? Besides, that was last week; this week it's elephant trainer."

"You're nuts."

"No. I'm going to train elephants for the police force like they do in India. Hey! Can you see a cop on an elephant in Central Park? 'Pick up that cigarette butt, mister, or I'll stomp on your head and turn it into an ashtray.' . . . What else is wrong with me?"

"I don't know. . . . Maybe you're prejudiced—"

"Me!" Shaun said, stopping in the middle of the street.

"Let me finish! I mean, maybe you're prejudiced against girls. Like you keep making fun of them and, I don't know, all those dirty jokes you tell seem to be against girls."

Alan looked straight ahead as he said it. He was testing Shaun; he knew it. Testing to see what might happen if Shaun ever found out about Naomi. Or whether *he* could possibly tell Shaun. He slowed his pace a little; he wanted to finish this talk before they reached school.

Shaun seemed confused. "That's something *wrong* with me?"

"I guess so."

"Wow! Hey, Al, sweetie-sweet, you got a *girl* friend or something?"

"No!"

"You know, you're acting kind of funny this morning. That's the screwiest thing to say that's wrong with someone that I ever heard of. You show me a girl who can hit a ball two hundred feet, and she can be on the team. But all they're good for is giggling. All they do is stand at the curb and watch the game and giggle."

"Well, maybe they do," said Alan, defensively. "But that's their way of kidding around, that's all."

"I'll bet you're hanging around with girls. La-de-da, sweetie-sweet. I'll bet you're playing hopscotch with them, sweetie-sweet. Or worse. Bet?"

"You're on! How much?"

"Two dollars. But I hope like hell I lose, believe it or not."

"Don't worry," said Alan. "You will."

"Good. 'Cause I ain't hanging around with no sissies. Not me."

Alan felt it as if it were a blow to the small of his back.
He had to keep Naomi a complete secret, that was clear.

But how could he have errands every day? He'd have
to think of an excuse that was airtight.

5

Alan searched in the kitchen for a brown paper bag to hide the Charlie McCarthy dummy. He didn't want anyone to see it on his short trip up to the Liebmans'. A dummy was all right for an eight-year-old, but at twelve and a half, it meant you were playing with dolls, unless it was connected to a magic show, or you were so good at it that you really were a super-terrific ventriloquist, like Edgar Bergen.

Outside, he could hear the shouts of the stickball game. The thought of what he was missing made him bite the side of his lip.

"So now what is it, Alan?" his mother asked. Alan winced a little; she could read every change in his face, no matter how slight.

"Nothing." He glanced toward the open window, then looked down.

"Oh," his mother said, seeing the glance. "What can I do? Alan, I'm sorry. It can't be helped." She went over and gently closed the window.

"You can at *least* get me a paper bag for this dummy.

So I don't look like a three-year-old baby out in the hall-way."

"I'm out of grocery bags. I needed them for the gar-bage. Can't you wrap it up in a newspaper?"

"No. I'd look like a nut carrying this thing in a news-paper."

"I don't have any more bags. . . . How about maybe in a suitcase?"

"What!"

"Or a . . . wait . . . the laundry bag. You could put it in the laundry bag."

"I'll take a newspaper," Alan said in despair.

With Charlie McCarthy wrapped in yesterday's head-lines, Alan slipped out of his apartment, looked down the hallway, then raced up the stairs to the next floor.

There was a smell of ammonia; Alan knew it meant the superintendent was washing the tiled floor. And sure enough, Finch was on his knees scrubbing at the far end of the hallway.

"Hey!" Finch called. "Don't go there! I just cleaned. It's still wet! You kids! Always making trouble! This isn't your floor! Get down to your floor! Why you making trouble, always, hah?"

"I have to give this to the Liebmans," Alan said in his weakest voice.

"You can't walk there! It's wet!"

Alan remembered his mother saying Finch was just a crank, and not to worry about his threats. He took a deep breath, walked straight to the Liebmans' door, and rang the bell.

"I'll tell your father! I'll tell the landlord! You kids! You'll be forced out of here! You'll see! I'm telling the landlord!"

Mrs. Liebman opened her door and stared at Mr. Finch. She was a most mild-mannered woman, but she was tall and heavy, and her stares were deadly when needed. Finch stared back for as long as he could, his eyes red with anger and ammonia fumes, but Mrs. Liebman won. Finch went back to his scrubbing, muttering "Kids" under his breath.

"Come in, please, Alan, you are so good, so kind to come. I can't say from my heart enough thank-you's. Your mother knows it, your father knows it, so please come in, come in."

She ushered Alan into the living room and pointed out a chair for him in front of an enormous bowl of fruit.

"Eat something, please," she said, taking an apple and holding it toward Alan.

"I . . . I'm not hungry, thanks."

"Maybe a pear? A banana? Alan, take. Whenever I'm by you, your mother is always with the food. So please, take."

"No, thanks."

A woman came into the living room from one of the bedrooms; it was Naomi's mother. Against Mrs. Liebman's large figure, the woman looked thin, almost emaciated, but her eyes were as large as Naomi's. She reminded Alan of a woman who sold pencils near the el station years ago, in all kinds of weather. There was that same pleading in her eyes.

"This is Mrs. Kirshenbaum, Alan. Naomi's mother," said Mrs. Liebman. Then she turned to Mrs. Kirshenbaum and said softly, "This is the boy."

"*Merci. Merci bien, Alan. Merci bien,*" said Mrs. Kirshenbaum, her eyes filling with tears.

Everybody keeps crying, thought Alan. They're *all* crazy.

"I see you brought something," said Mrs. Liebman, pointing to the bundle in Alan's arm. "It's not frightening, is it?"

"No. It's just . . . something for us to do."

"All right. She's in her bedroom. It's important, Alan, to be very calm. To not move quickly. And not to go too close. It frightens her. You understand?"

"Yes."

"An apple first? A pear?"

"No, thanks. I'm really not—you know—hungry."

"So . . . In Switzerland, Alan, she was also sick. She had bad dreams; she screamed at night. But she got better; much better. She studied at home. She's a very bright girl, Alan. Very, very bright. Like you. Your mother tells me all about you. Why do you think we've asked you? You understand?"

What did his mother *say* about him, Alan wondered. Why did she always have to talk about him?

Mrs. Liebman shook her head, lost in her own thoughts. "Now she's somewhere else most of the time. She has to wake up from it. *Oy, Gott,* what can I tell you! Alan, come. . . ."

Mrs. Liebman walked to the bedroom door and opened

it very gently. Mrs. Kirshenbaum stood behind them, uncertain whether to go to the door or not. Naomi was sitting cross-legged on her bed, tearing a piece of paper into tiny bits. They stood watching her for a moment.

Like in the zoo, thought Alan. The Central Park Zoo. Watching that monkey that day, tearing his food to shreds. For a half second, he felt they were all watching an animal in the zoo. There even seemed to be a smell. Horrible, this watching. *Horrible!*

Then Alan walked slowly into the room and sat on a chair by the door. Naomi kept concentrating on the paper she was tearing. Mrs. Liebman and Mrs. Kirshenbaum went back to the living room, listening for the slightest sound of alarm.

Alan decided to start right away with Charlie McCarthy. He unwrapped the dummy, and at the sound of crinkling paper, Naomi looked up.

Alan made the dummy wave its arm. Naomi immediately reached under her pillow and pulled out the doll. It was ragged and old, as if it had been through many troubles.

Naomi made the doll wave back. Monkey see, monkey do, thought Alan.

"My name is Charlie McCarthy," Alan made the dummy say. "Hello, kid. How are they treating you here?"

Naomi made the doll pick up the piece of paper, then started tearing the paper between the doll's hands, as if the doll were doing it.

"Hey, kid," said the dummy. "I can do that. That's

38

easy." Alan made his dummy tear bits of the *New York Times* wrapping. Naomi looked up several times and, satisfied that there was no danger, continued to make the doll tear the paper.

After five minutes, Alan decided he'd better try something else. They'd be tearing up paper all afternoon. It was so boring, and his fingers were beginning to ache.

"I can dance, you know," Alan made Charlie say. "Watch!" Alan started singing "Roll out the barrel . . ." while making the dummy dance.

The doll kept tearing the paper, but every so often, Naomi stopped to watch Charlie McCarthy's antics. Suddenly, Alan made him dance upside down, bouncing him up and down on his head and—yes, Naomi seemed to smile a little, just the slightest reluctant crease, as if she were fighting desperately against it. But a trace of a smile had slipped out. Alan tried not to look too eager as he made the dummy dance all over the room.

The paper tearing continued. Alan made the dummy dance sideways on the wall, but Naomi had stopped looking up, and the smile didn't reappear.

Well, at least she isn't afraid of me anymore, Alan thought. If she won't do anything else but tear paper up, it isn't my fault, is it? But how can anyone tear up pieces of paper so much! She's crazy, that's what, and I'll never be able to do any good, and it's not fair!

Alan took the dummy and started wrapping it in the newspaper, while the doll kept tearing and tearing. Then Mrs. Liebman came into the room, silently holding out a Hershey bar toward Alan. Mrs. Liebman seemed to be begging him to take it as she pressed it toward him.

Alan took the bar of chocolate and mumbled, "Thanks." Just like in a zoo, thought Alan. Feed the animals. OK, Charlie, *you* eat it. He slipped it into the package with the dummy. Then he took a last look at Naomi still tearing, and said, "Hey, kid, I'll see you tomorrow, OK? Tomorrow I'm going to teach you how to be a ventriloquist. OK? . . . OK? . . . So long, kid."

But it was as if he were speaking to an empty room.

6

It rained the next day, a gloomy New York rain that turned the classroom windows into dismal gray mirrors. There would be no stickball that afternoon. On the way home from school Alan celebrated his release from another round of "errand" excuses by leaping straight into a shallow lake formed by a clogged sewer.

"Come on!" he shouted to Shaun. "Let's go swimming!"

Alan slammed his foot down in the water, trying to hit Shaun at the curb, and the water fight was on. It quickly turned into a Pacific battle scene.

"OK, Kelly, here comes the Grumman Hellcat! I'm knocking out your last aircraft carrier." Alan kicked up a shower of water, as if a bomb had fallen. "Carroongh! It's a hit."

"My Zero's heading down your smokestack, Silverman! Right down your smokestack! Take that! Kachanggg! Your boiler room's exploded, Yankee pig!"

"You can't! I just hit your Zero!" Alan shouted.

"I've got another! They keep coming!" Shaun kicked water at Alan again and again, as the fight raged.

Within ten minutes, they were both so wet that they no longer noticed the rain. In the grand finale, Shaun slipped and fell, soaking his pants and shirt right through his raincoat.

"Yeaaa! We won back the Philippines!" shouted Alan.

"I surrender, Yankee dog!" said Shaun. "I now commit honorable hari-kari." Shaun made a motion to cut himself across the stomach, but instead scooped a fountain of water up over Alan's head.

"Banzai!" Shaun called.

"Geronimo!" Alan answered, kicking one final bombardment of water at Shaun.

They headed toward home, soaked pants clinging to their legs, wet shoes squeaking in their rubbers. Once inside the apartment lobby, Alan took special joy in getting Finch's tiled floor soaking wet. He took off his raincoat and shook it out like a toreador's cape.

"Hey, Kelly, how about a bullfight?" he asked.

"Not me. I'm freezing," said Shaun, as he pushed open the lobby door.

Alan shivered in his soaked clothes, but he didn't want to admit he was cold. "Freezing? The great Shaun Kelly? Come on, I'll race you to the roof."

"Tomorrow," said Shaun, as he let the lobby door squeal slowly back.

Alan dashed through the narrowing gap and up the stairs, past Shaun. "You lost," he called as he sped toward his apartment.

"You're really nuts, Silverman!" Shaun called from below.

"You're all wet, Kelly! Nobody listens to someone who's all wet."

Alan opened his apartment door quietly and tried to slip past the kitchen, but his mother was there, arms folded, at the door. One look at Alan was all she needed.

"Get a towel! Two towels! Six-year-old! Take off the shoes! Take off the socks! Get dry quick, or it's pneumonia. A six-year-old, I have. Why do you *do* things like this?"

"What'd I do?"

"Look at yourself! Look at your books! What do you think, I was born yesterday? You think I can't tell you were wrestling in the rainstorm with that Kelly?"

"His name's Shaun!"

"I don't care if his name is Yankee Doodle! He's a hoodlum!"

"He is not!"

"Just wait! One day . . ."

"One day, what? What do you think he's gonna do, blow up a bank? . . . In case you want to know, *I* started it."

"Started what?"

"The water fight."

"See! There *was* a fight!"

"So *I'm* the hoodlum."

"You? Some hoodlum. You wouldn't hurt a fly. Everybody tells me what a lovely son I have. And Mrs. Liebman is so—"

"STOP THAT!"

"What is it? Alan? What?" His mother looked alarmed.

"I'm not *lovely!*"

"All right, all right. I agree; you're not lovely. So help me, you're not."

"You bet I'm not! And stop talking about me to people!"

"All right, all right. . . . Alan, you're not forgetting . . ." His mother gestured upward toward the Liebmans' apartment.

"I know. You don't have to tell me."

Alan took a towel from the bathroom and went to his room. As he dried himself, he wondered whether he *had* been trying to forget about Naomi. Maybe that's why he'd started the water fight: to delay his visit as long as he could. If only Mrs. Liebman and Mrs. Kirshenbaum would stay away and not push fruit toward him and thank him with Hershey bars and cry all over the place. . . .

Alan sat at his desk and carefully examined his flying model of a Piper Cub for new tears in the tissue-paper skin. Maybe he and Shaun could fly this Saturday if the weather cleared. Then he realized he was delaying again.

But it felt good to just sit there with the plane. Why can't I, he thought. I *like* sitting here. Who wants to sit in a room with someone who's crazy? And you can't even get angry at her, because you're not allowed to. Because she's crazy. The whole thing is crazy! You can't play ball; you can't fool around in the rain; you can't just sit and look at your planes; no! You can't do anything except go upstairs and sit in a room with a crazy girl you can't even get angry at! What a job!

Alan sighed. He studied the plane for another minute, then went to the closet and took out the Charlie McCarthy dummy.

"Here we go again, Charlie. Are you ready?"

"I was just starting a good nap, Mr. Bergen."

"Too bad. It's time for work."

"Work! I'll give you a kick in the teeth, Bergen."

After wrapping the dummy in the same newspaper, Alan went to the kitchen.

"OK. I'm going up." He held up the newspaper package for his mother to see.

"Don't you want a hot chocolate first?" his mother asked.

"No, thanks."

"All right. Then if you catch pneumonia, it's not my fault. Did you change, at least?"

"Yes. So long." Then from his newspaper package he made the dummy say, "So long, toots."

"What?"

"That was McCarthy. He's a hoodlum, too."

"Meshuggener!"

"What'd the lady say?" Alan made the dummy ask.

"She said you're crazy, Charlie."

"Not *him*," said Alan's mother. *"You!"*

Alan opened his front door and checked the hallway. No one. He ran upstairs and hurried to the Liebman apartment.

Mrs. Liebman offered Alan fruit and soda, and this time Alan decided a cherry soda would help make Mrs.

Liebman feel that he didn't hate her food. Besides, he was thirsty.

He went quietly into Naomi's room and set the glass of soda down. Naomi was sitting on her bed, surrounded by crumpled bits of paper. She stared at a piece of wrinkled paper in her hand. Every few moments she shrugged her shoulders as if to say "I don't care."

Alan unwrapped the dummy and made it talk, but Naomi didn't even look up. Then she started tearing the crumpled paper, shrugging every so often.

It's no use, thought Alan. I'm wasting my time. It's almost worse than yesterday. She doesn't even have that dumb doll of hers.

"Hey, kid. Where's my friend you had yesterday?" asked Charlie. "Why don't you get her?"

Naomi turned away and continued tearing. She didn't care at all, about anything! Here he was trying his best, and she didn't even care! Like when his mother . . .

Alan tried to recall the time his newborn sister had died, and his mother had sat alone all day in the bedroom when she came home from the hospital. She hadn't seemed to care about anyone or anything.

"Just keep talking," his father had said. "Keep talking, Alan, and she'll hear you."

He had hated it! He remembered, now, how much he'd hated it! His mother sitting there with her head down! Not caring about anyone, not about him, his father, anyone.

But it *had* worked: talking to her as if she were listening. By evening, she'd come out to the kitchen, very sadly, and forced herself to prepare dinner. And after that, she was fine, or seemed to be.

But that had been one day! Naomi seemed to be like this all the time. It was hopeless.

Still, it *had* worked for his mother, and he *had* promised. Alan forced himself to make Charlie appear happy and bubbly and full of fun. But it was with the same sinking feeling he had when he knew he was losing a chess game but had to keep playing. And at the end, Naomi was still tearing tiny bits from that same crumpled piece of paper. Hopeless.

7

Shaun held his cupped hand high in the air, following the white moth flickering among weeds. Then his hand dropped like a hawk to its prey, and the moth was under it. The butterfly bombardment was under way. Only the butterflies weren't butterflies; they were moths.

"Careful," Alan called. "You're crushing him."

"I am not! I know how to catch moths, for crying out loud!"

"Its wings will tear. They can tear from almost anything."

On the way to school that morning, Shaun had told Alan about his greatest idea in months: the butterfly bombardment. They would capture dozens of butterflies during the noon hour in the huge empty lot two blocks from the school. Then they'd release the butterflies during Mrs. Landley's English class. Alan had hesitated; Mrs. Landley was his favorite teacher, even though he thought she gushed too much. But Shaun had started using the word "sissy" again, and Alan had decided to go along with Shaun and worry about Mrs. Landley later.

"OK," said Shaun, holding his hand over the moth. "Get the bag and turn it upside down above my hand. Come on!"

Alan unfolded the brown paper bag he'd used for his lunch and put it over Shaun's hand. Shaun turned his cupped hand upward and made a throwing motion into the bag.

"Go on! Fly! . . . He won't go," said Shaun.

"Because you probably crushed him."

Shaun released the moth, and they watched it flutter wildly in little white circles.

"He's hurt all right," said Shaun. "He can't fly. Put him out of his misery. Kill him, Alan."

"Why *me*? You did it!"

"You mean you won't even kill a moth? Boy, you *are* nuts."

"I don't feel like killing it, that's all. Besides, it's your moth, now."

Alan remembered how angry his mother became when he would scoop up a roach and throw it out the front door rather than kill it. "Look at him," she would call. "He cares more about insects, this one, than some people care about people. That's why there's so many roaches."

Shaun raised his foot above the moth. "OK, Silverman. Here goes. You can kiss him good-bye." The moth fluttered and paused, fluttered and paused. Shaun hesitated, then lowered his foot.

"Well, maybe we don't actually have to kill him," said Shaun, as he gently took the moth and set it on a leaf. Then he pulled some brown woolen fuzz from his sweater and put it in front of the moth. "There! Maybe he'll eat that. . . . Yeah, go ahead and eat it. Go ahead, little fella. Eat it."

Alan looked at Shaun in amazement. Shaun of the rope-tight muscles and quick fists was talking to a moth. Cared about a moth; cared about an insect the same as *he* did.

"Hey, that's great, Kelly," said Alan. "He likes you."

Shaun looked at Alan, his eyes narrowing. "You tell this to any of the guys and I'll knock three of your teeth out, Silverman. I mean it!"

"I won't tell anybody. But I'm glad you didn't kill him, OK?"

Shaun shrugged. "OK."

"Let's get back to school," said Alan.

"What do you mean! We still have to do the butterfly bombardment. Only this time, you do the catching and I'll hold the bag open. You've got daintier hands, Silverman. . . . Hey, there's one. Let's get him, Al. What are you waiting for? Don't you know how to hunt? Come on!"

They moved quickly from one patch of weeds to another, and within fifteen minutes, they had two bags with several dozen moths in each. They punched holes in the bags with a pencil to give the moths air, then walked back to school with the bags held out like brown lanterns. Alan thought he could feel the moths fluttering against the crinkly paper.

In English class, Alan and Shaun hid their paper bags under their desks, covering them with their sweaters. At the right moment, Shaun was to give the signal for releasing the bombardment: a fake sneeze.

"Now class," said Mrs. Landley, "where were we yesterday? Let me think. I believe we were in the middle of Emily Dickinson. Let's see, page eighty-nine. We did the 'My life closed twice before its close' poem, didn't we? No? Ralph? Did we? . . . Yes we did. Good. Well, that poem was a very serious one, as we discussed. What closed twice? Do you remember? Norma?"

"Guys she loved."

There was a burst of giggles in the classroom.

"Yes," said Mrs. Landley. "Well, it was love itself that she'd lost. The loss of love can be tragic. Is tragic. Always. The loss of someone we love. You look doubtful, Shaun."

"Huh? N-no . . ." Shaun stammered. Alan could see from across the room that Shaun's neck had turned slightly pink.

"All right. That was a serious poem. But Emily Dickinson isn't always serious. Let's try the next one. Larry Dennison, would you try it. Middle of the page."

Larry started reading the poem, slowly, carefully, pausing after every line, as he always did. " 'A bird came down the walk' . . . mm . . . 'He did not know I saw' . . . umm . . . 'He bit an angleworm in halves' . . . uh . . . 'And ate the fellow, raw. . . .' "

Alan, impatient, read ahead through the poem. What was this! In the last stanza: butterflies! Emily Dickinson had said something about butterflies. If I can only open the bag at the right second, he thought. Shaun, forget about your dopey sneeze! Read the poem! Get the bombardment ready!

Larry continued his reading, while Alan took the bag out from under his desk, his hands clumsy with excitement. He looked at Shaun hopefully, but Shaun didn't see him. Alan tried a fake sneeze of his own. "Ker-auff!"

Shaun didn't notice.

" 'Than oars divide the ocean . . .' " Larry continued reading. "Umm . . . 'Too silver for a seam' . . . mmm . . . 'Or butterflies, off banks of noon' . . . umm . . . 'Leap, plashless as they swim.' "

On the word "butterflies," Alan opened his bag and shook it. Like feathers bursting from a torn pillow, the moths were everywhere at once.

Shaun rushed to open his bag, but in the uproar no one noticed him. Mrs. Landley appeared stunned by the butterfly bombardment. She shook her head again and again as she gazed at the moths.

What had he done! She was his favorite teacher in the whole stupid school. But now she'd think he was a troublemaker. Why didn't she say something?

Suddenly, Mrs. Landley rapped on her desk with a paperweight, for attention. The class was instantly still. Alan knew it meant the principal's office, at least, and a note home to be signed. At least!

"Class," said Mrs. Landley, "in all my years of teaching, I have never seen such a perfectly beautiful way of celebrating a poem. All poems. It is absolutely moving. To release these beautiful creatures is itself an act of poetry. You knew this poem was coming, didn't you, Alan. Yes, you're always ahead of the rest of us. Beautiful! Thank you, Alan, for this lovely gift. It almost makes me want to fly away like the bird in the poem. And those sweet butterflies."

A boy called out in a high falsetto voice, "And sweet Alan. He's a butterfly, too."

Alan tasted the anger in him rising. The boy was Carl Newman. Carl made fun of anyone he could, whenever he could. As some others in the class tittered, Alan glanced back toward Shaun. It couldn't be! Shaun was laughing, too! When he saw Alan staring at him, Shaun sobered up and shrugged at Alan. Alan turned away and bit his lip.

"All right, that's quite enough, class!" Mrs. Landley called. "I expect better from this group. The Rapid Advance class indeed! Rapid ignorance, I'd say! Someone please open the windows and let the butterflies go home. You don't deserve them."

Alan avoided Shaun as the class walked single file from English to the general science room. But in the science laboratory, Shaun moved over to Alan's workbench and whispered, "Hey, Silverman, you were great! No one else could have gotten away with it! Stop being such a sorehead."

"Go to hell!" Alan whispered back.

"Goo goo."

"It was all your idea, and you just sat and laughed! At *me*!" Alan concentrated on his experiment, not looking at Shaun.

"So what? People laugh at *me* sometimes."

"People, maybe, but not friends!"

"Oh . . . Well, OK, I'm sorry. OK?"

Alan sighed and kept working. "OK." Was he really sorry, Alan wondered.

"See you after school," Shaun whispered.

"Can't. Got an errand."

"Again?"

"Again."

Later that day, as he sat in Naomi's room with Charlie, Alan wondered about Shaun. Why did Shaun change from one minute to the next? Is that how friends were? Sometimes friends and sometimes almost enemies? His mother seemed like that, but she was a mother, not a friend. Joe Condello was always an enemy. Tony Ferrara was usually neither; he was just sort of there.

Alan watched Naomi. She wasn't even *there*. She was nowhere at all. She'd taken out her doll again, but only to use it for tearing up endless bits of paper. Alan had put Charlie through all his songs and jokes, but nothing had worked. He'd even made Charlie do some magic tricks.

Alan decided it was time to go. "OK," he made Charlie say, "I've got to get back to my beautiful, big, luxurious closet where I live in super splendor. This is Charlie McCarthy saying so long, friends. Signing off. Over and out. Roger. Wilco. Good-bye."

Then, hesitantly, without looking up, Naomi turned the doll toward the dummy and made it say, in a high, squeaky doll's voice, "Ah, Sharlee. . . . You visit again . . . *non*? . . . Next time I dance, *aussi*. . . . I am Yvette . . . and I'm good *danseuse*. . . . As good like Pavlova, even. . . . *Au revoir*, Sharlee . . . Mack-artee."

Naomi turned the doll back and continued the paper tearing. Her face was completely blank, as if nothing had happened.

But something *had* happened. A dozen things had happened all at once. She was a girl, not an animal in the zoo! She had understood Charlie McCarthy's name! Her doll had a name: Yvette! Her words made sense, too. Except, who was Pavlova? And what did *"aussi"* mean? Was it a dance? Hadn't they learned a word like that in French class? *Ici? Aussi?* It didn't really matter. It was great! He wasn't in an empty room any longer.

Alan took a breath and made Charlie say, "So long Naom— I mean, Yvette. See you tomorrow."

Naomi opened her mouth slightly as she licked her lip in total concentration on the work of tearing.

"*Au revoir*, kid," said Charlie.

Naomi said nothing.

Well, maybe it's enough for now, thought Alan. He went back to the living room with the dummy half wrapped. He could see that Naomi's mother and Mrs. Liebman had heard Naomi's high-pitched doll's voice. And Alan knew it had been good; their eyes were shining like newly washed pebbles.

"I'll be back tomorrow," said Alan. "OK?"

Alan tried to move away, but Mrs. Liebman rushed over and kissed him on his forehead.

"Like my own son," she said. "You should be blessed."

Oh good grief, thought Alan.

8

Naomi didn't speak. Saturday, Sunday, she sat with her doll, Yvette, and made the doll tear sheets of paper. Twice Naomi put on the doll's shoes, only to take them off again, immediately. Several times, when Charlie was singing and dancing, Alan thought he heard Naomi humming the same tune in that high doll's voice, humming for Yvette. Alan strained to hear, but the thin voice seemed to be less than an echo, disappearing instantly when he stopped to listen. Was it there at all?

It was a dark, sad week. The rain returned, an endless drizzle that even umbrellas couldn't stop for long. It seemed to rain upward, into the sky. Alan remembered his grandmother's funeral in such a rain, the black umbrellas clustered and touching, forming a tent of mourning by the grave. The umbrellas seemed to be in mourning, again. It was a miserable week.

Monday, Tuesday, Wednesday, Alan visited Naomi. He made Charlie build picket fences with dominoes that collapsed from left to right, at a touch. Did Naomi smile at that a little? She seemed to, so he tried it again. And again. And again. She didn't smile. She hadn't smiled. He'd been mistaken.

He made a parachute from a handkerchief and string. His house key became the aviator who had bailed out. Naomi looked up once, and watched the parachute billow out as it sank to the floor. The key clinked as it hit. Naomi shrugged and returned to her paper tearing.

Nothing worked. Nothing *would* work! How many times did they expect him to come up here like this? How many games and toys and tricks did he have left?

"It's raining, anyway," his mother had said several times. "You can mope upstairs by her instead of in your room, yes?"

All right. But wait till the sun comes out, he thought. Just wait.

On Thursday morning the heavy gray sky began to pull apart like wet paper, and jagged seams of blue appeared. By noontime the sun was out, opening like a flower to a thousand petals of light. It was autumn again, clean and clear, and Shaun was shouting to Alan about stickball. Was he going to play today, after school?

And Alan, smelling the sun and the sky, said yes, he'd be there, he'd be ready right after school. He decided he wouldn't even go upstairs to his apartment. It was going to be stickball, not Naomi. He'd had enough of Naomi and her beat-up doll, and her scraps of paper, and her dumb face. It was going to be stickball, period!

That afternoon there was none of the usual arguing over sides; after all that rain, everyone was eager to just start playing. The remaining puddles were declared out-of-bounds, and they began.

It felt good to be swinging a stickball bat again, to connect even for a foul ball, to be cheered by Shaun.

"Attaboy, Alan, baby! Straighten it out now! Down the middle, Alan, baby! Knock it over the roof!"

Condello looked toward first as he always did, even though there was no one on first, then shot the ball toward the plate. Alan swung and twisted around. He'd struck out.

Alan banged the bat against the pavement, then dropped it and walked to the curb. *SILVERMAN BACK IN LINEUP. SPRAINED WRIST AND TORN LIGA-MENT CAUSE PAIN AT BAT. CROWD CHEERS HERO AS HE STRIKES OUT.*

Alan dropped a pop fly in the following inning, missing an easy out. And his next time at bat, he struck out again.

He was playing miserably! Why? Not enough practice? Or was he just a rotten player? Everyone else seemed sharper. True, the street was still wet and it slowed up the game, but it was wet for everyone.

In his third time at bat, he struck out again. Three times in a row.

"Raay, Silverman!" one of the boys on the other team called. "You're *our* best player!"

"Lay off!" shouted Shaun.

It was that "lay off" that hurt the most. As if he needed protection. As if he were some sort of delicate flower. He wished he could walk away from the game. Just quit. But he couldn't. He had to look as if he didn't care. The way the players looked at Yankee Stadium. But inside he wanted to scream. Did they feel that way at Yankee Stadium when they struck out three times in a row?

His team lost, five to two. As Alan walked upstairs, his mind suddenly shifted from stickball to his mother and father. What would they say about his skipping Naomi?

But he deserved a day of stickball! He deserved it! He didn't care what they said! He deserved it!

Alan walked in and stood at the kitchen door. His mother and father abruptly dropped their conversation.

"So?" said his mother. "You don't even come upstairs from school anymore?"

"I . . ." Alan shifted his books. "I took a day off, OK? I think I can have a day off, once in a million years."

"True, true," said his father. "But you could tell your mother, couldn't you? Upstairs, they were waiting for you."

"She wouldn't have let me take a day off. And neither would you!"

"All right, look, you took an afternoon off," his father said. "And you didn't tell us. Terrible! Ten years in the clink on bread and water."

"Sol, you're making it into a joke!" said Alan's mother, her voice rising.

"He's not in the Army. We can't tell him that if he takes an afternoon off, someone may lose a battle. Or even a war. He's not a soldier. Right, Alan? You're just Alan. Plain and simple."

"Can I at least put down my books?" Alan asked.

"Why not? It's your constitutional right. . . . As I

was saying, you're just Alan, not a soldier. But you *are* my son, and I'm your father. As your father, I forgive you ten times over for playing stickball. And I hope, as my son, you'll forgive me five times over for telling you that now I expect you to go upstairs. Eat something. There's some cold chicken in the refrigerator. We've finished supper. Eat the chicken, then go upstairs to Naomi."

"But . . . but what about my homework? I have a test in math tomorrow!"

"Very simple. You'll fail the test. Eat the chicken, Alan, and go upstairs."

"But—"

"No buts! You can study when you come down, and get less sleep. That's up to you. I have to be tough sometimes, Alan, or else you'll never become . . . yourself."

"You're always tough! On me! Only on me!"

"Watch how you talk to your father with that mouth of—"

"It's all right," his father interrupted. "I'm sorry, Alan, but I have to do what I think is right. What I *think*. I'm not sure, but I think. You're much more than a stickball player. If you were only a stickball player, I wouldn't bother. You're a person. A *mensh*. Eat the chicken, already, before I give you heartburn, or the mumps."

Alan ate a few bites of chicken, but there was a tangle of feelings in him twisting like a basketful of snakes. He couldn't eat.

He went upstairs with the dummy and sat in a corner of Naomi's bedroom. She sat as usual, making Yvette, the doll, tear bits of paper.

His father was right. He *wasn't* a stickball player, that was for sure. And the boys knew it. They knew it. He wasn't a stickball player, and he wasn't a *mensh,* a man, and he wasn't a person. He was a nothing! He was good in school, but so what? Sissies were good in school. All he could do was read books, but he'd never be like the people he read about. The first mate of the *Bounty.* The Count of Monte Cristo. Edison. Ben Hur. Ty Cobb. None.

He was as much of a nothing as . . . as Naomi. Why was she looking at him? Because he was as crazy as she was? Crazy people can tell that others are crazy, right? And he *was* crazy. He wasn't like the other boys. What other boy in his right mind would sit here in this screwball room with a dummy and a doll and a crazy girl? He wasn't like the other boys. He wondered if he was a boy at all. Maybe it was some sort of trick. Maybe he was a girl. The thought horrified him: maybe that's why they picked him for Naomi!

He *was* going crazy. Why was she *looking* at him? Could she tell what he was thinking? The doll had stopped tearing paper.

"Why are you . . . so sad, Sharlee . . . *pourquoi?*" Yvette asked. The high squeaky doll's voice came in little bursts, like the call of a young bird still afraid of itself.

"*Pauvre Sharlee* . . . do not be crying . . ." the doll said softly.

She was talking again! What had he done? Nothing! Make Charlie say something, idiot!

He raised the dummy to sitting position. "Hey, Yvette, kid, I'm not crying. See. *Bonjour, Yvette.*"

"Comment ça va . . . Sharlee?"

"Huh? What's that mean?"

"How are you . . . Sharlee?" Yvette squeaked.

"I'm great, Yvette, kid. How are you?" said Charlie. She was talking! Sensible talk! Like a human being! Naomi-Yvette.

"Voilà. My slippers for . . . for ballet," said Yvette, still hesitant. Naomi took the doll's shoes and put them on Yvette's feet. "You dance . . . with me, Sharlee? I dance . . . if you dance . . . ."

"Sure. OK," said Charlie. "Here we go, Naomi."

Naomi instantly leaped to the farthest part of her bed, away from Alan. Fear spread from her mouth to her eyes. Yvette asked, in a tight, shrill voice, "Naomi! Who is *that?*"

Alan blinked and hesitated. Stupid jerk, he thought. It's supposed to be Charlie to *Yvette.* Jerk! Say the right thing now.

"I meant . . . let's dance, Yvette, kid. . . ."

"Non!"

"Please?"

But Naomi was taking off the doll's shoes again. And in a moment, she had started the doll tearing a scrap of paper.

"Tomorrow, then. Yvette, will you dance with me tomorrow?"

The doll tore and tore, while Naomi's face remained blank. Alan felt those snakes in his stomach twisting again. It was like another strikeout, if she didn't answer. Like ten strikeouts in a row. Couldn't he do *anything* right?

"Yvette, please, tomorrow? Will you dance with me, Yvette?"

There was another moment's pause, then Yvette said very softly, *"Oui. Demain soir. . . ."*

"Huh?" Alan tried to recall his French. "Uh . . . Evening? Tomorrow evening?"

"Oui." The doll continued tearing.

"Great! I'll see you *demain soir*, Yvette. *Au revoir.*"

"Au revoir, Sharlee," said the doll.

Alan gave a loud sigh. It had been close, but he hadn't struck out after all. Maybe he'd even won a battle, or something, for his father tonight. There *was* a Naomi there; that was for sure. But she was as hard to catch and hold as a shiny droplet of mercury.

9

They were at the airfield, or what was left of the airfield. Holmes Airport was over two miles from Alan's house, but on Saturdays when the wind was right, Alan and Shaun took their flying models out to Holmes. Shaun had a Stinson Reliant, and Alan a Piper Cub.

Years ago, Alan had seen parachute demonstrations at the airport, and a flying circus, and air races. The busy planes, yellow and red, had circled and roared like angry tigers. But now there were weeds on the airfield, and all that was left of the musical planes and the goggled men was the smell of engine oil soaked into the earth.

Shaun and Alan ran along the airstrip toward the far end, the end where the wind sock once stood.

"Hey!" Alan called. "The wind's just right!"

"Yeah, it's my kind of wind!" Shaun called back. "Ten cents says my plane stays up longer than yours, first flight."

"I won't bet!"

"OK. Then it's a thousand dollars!"

As Shaun and Alan wound their propellers, the long rubber bands that powered the planes knotted and re-knotted into twisted ropes. Alan held his plane aloft and imagined it to be a real one. *THEY'RE READY FOR THE TAKEOFF. A HUNDRED-MILE RACE, WIN-NER TAKE ALL. SILVERMAN NUMBER FIVE IN THE PIPER. KELLY NUMBER EIGHT IN THE STINSON. READY. REMOVE WHEEL CHOCKS! CONTACT!*

The planes rose and turned precisely, like birds wheel-ing toward a distant home. The wings dipped and re-covered with every new layer of wind.

"Look at her go!"

"Mine's higher, Silverman!"

The wind seemed to be a living thing, a great friendly creature playing with the airplanes, rough play, gentle play. The planes landed perfectly, set down like rare gifts before them.

They flew the planes for another hour, then decided to lie back on the ground and watch for real planes, before going home. A sea gull, straying from Long Island Sound, moved overhead in a lazy half circle.

"Look at that gull," said Alan. "That's how they de-signed the Spitfire. He watched gulls, the designer." Alan cupped his eyes, trying to follow the soaring bird.

"I saw that movie," said Shaun. "They made it all up. You can't design anything from watching birds. . . . I don't see any planes. Let's go. Maybe we can get up a stickball game."

"Hey, that's an idea! I can play today! . . . I can't

play weekdays anymore, though."

"What! How come? What's going on?"

"It's that errand. It's sort of a permanent errand on weekdays. Saturdays, I can do this errand whenever I want, but . . . Anyway, it's kind of a family thing. Sort of a secret."

"Is your father a drunk or something?"

"My father? I don't think he's ever drunk anything in his life, except maybe wine on Passover."

"What's Passover?"

"A holiday. It comes around Easter. It's when the ancient Hebrews escaped from Egypt."

"Oh . . . And people drink wine? That's a pretty good holiday. How many bottles do they drink?"

"They just sip some with the Seder. It's a kind of feast. It's like Thanksgiving, that's what. We visit my grand-parents usually. Like I guess you probably do on Easter, right?"

"My grandfather is still in Ireland," said Shaun. "I've never seen him. . . . Anyway, what's the big secret you can't tell me?"

"That's just it. I can't tell you, that's all."

But inside, Alan ached to tell. If only he could. It would be easier, much easier. Shaun could help him; he could do all sorts of things. He knew how to play the harmonica; he could teach Naomi. And if there were *two* of them, how could anyone call Alan a sissy? Could he tell him? Or would Shaun just call him a name, like Sweet Butter-fly, or something, and laugh like he had in class? Laugh along with the other boys, behind his back. . . . Well, maybe he *could* tell him. Shaun cared about moths; wouldn't he care about a person, for crying out loud? Sure he could tell him . . . maybe.

"Uh . . . Say, Shaun, I was going to ask. You know that girl who moved in on the top floor—"

"Who? Crazy Cat?"

"What? What do you mean, Crazy Cat?"

"Are you blind? Didn't you ever see her in the hallway, tearing up newspapers? She used to throw paper off the roof, till Finch chased her. She's crazy. All girls are crazy, she's just crazier, that's what. She's not even in school. I'll bet she sounds like a screwball when she talks, except you'd never know because it's all in French."

It was no use. He'd been right, all along. It wouldn't work, telling Shaun.

"I don't know," said Alan. "Maybe she can speak good English. Some kids learn English in Europe." He had to force himself not to reveal how much he knew about her. But it felt just like outright lying.

"I'll bet you ten dollars she can't say more than five words in English. That's two dollars a word. Bet?"

"No."

"That's because you know I'm right. Crazy Cat is really crazy."

"Why do you keep calling her that! Her name is Naomi . . . I heard."

"Oh, the Boy Scouts have landed," said Shaun. "Let's give this one a merit badge for nice-nice."

"If you call her Crazy Cat, pretty soon everybody will."

Shaun sat up again and studied Alan. Alan noticed

67

Shaun staring at him.

"What's wrong?" asked Alan.

"Nothing. Just wondering," Shaun answered. "Come on, let's head home. There's no planes around. Just Spitfires camouflaged to look like sea gulls."

10

That evening, Alan sensed that Naomi was better the moment he walked into her room. Her eyes looked brighter and she seemed ready to smile as she put on Yvette's shoes. Still, there were little bits of torn paper lying all over the floor.

"Hiya, Yvette, kid," Charlie said as Alan took the dummy out of the newspaper wrappings.

"Hiya?" asked Yvette. "What is 'hiya'?"

"How are you?" Alan made Charlie pronounce slowly.

"*Très bien.* Is dancing time, Sharlee," said Yvette in her doll's voice. "Come out from your newspapier—I mean, newspap*er*—and we dance, maybe, polka or a waltz, *oui*?"

It was great! Naomi was completely relaxed. No hesitation; nothing! His father had been right, after all. Keep talking! Keep talking!

"Hey, Yvette," said Charlie, "I can hardly speak French, but you speak very good English for a doll, you know."

"*Merci.* I learn from her."

"Who?"

"*Her! Her!*" Naomi made the doll gesture toward herself.

"Oh yeah, *her.*"

"Yeah? Yeah is 'yes,' *n'est-ce pas?*"

"*Oui.* I mean yes," said Charlie. "But you must be pretty smart, Yvette, to know all this English, huh?"

"*Eh bien,* I study English very hard three years in Switzerland," said the doll. "But it is *difficile*—I mean difficult—language."

"So's French. *He's* studying French in school," said Alan for the dummy, making it gesture toward himself.

"Oh. I can do good in that. I know plenty French."

"Yeah . . . I mean yes."

"I know plenty swear words in French," said Yvette, the doll.

"You do?"

"*Ah oui.*"

"Does *she* know any?" asked Charlie, pointing toward Naomi.

"*Non, non.* She's stupid. And dumb. She is *folle.*"

"*Folle?* Is that a swear word?"

"*Non.* Means crazy in the head."

Alan didn't quite know what to make the dummy say next. Did Naomi really know she was sort of . . . well, crazy?

"OK, Yvette, kid," said Charlie. "Let's do a dance."

"Uhkay."

"How about a tap dance?"

"Uhkay."

Alan started singing "Roll out the barrel . . ." and made the dummy hop up and down. Naomi made Yvette follow, and soon the dummy and the doll were dancing in great leaps from the bed, to the floor, to the dresser, and back. Then Alan turned Charlie over and made him bounce on his head. In a moment, Yvette was bouncing on her head, too.

"I think we're upside down," said Charlie.

"*Non, non,* I see your face very good. We both are right up.

"You mean right *side* up."

"*Oui*, right side up. It is the room, she is upside down."

"That's it! The house has turned over."

"The table is upside down."

"And the bed."

"Stupid room. It is dizzy."

And for the first time, Naomi laughed.

"Hey," Alan made Charlie call out, "I need a rest. You're some dancer, kid."

"You some dancer, too, keed," said Yvette.

"I am, I am. I'm terrific, 'cause I'm Charlie McCarthy. . . . Hey, I like you, Yvette."

"I like you, too, Sharlee. You are my boyfriend, *oui?*"

"I guess so. And you're my . . ." Alan found it difficult to say, even from the dummy to the doll. "Uh . . . girl friend, right?"

"*Ah oui.* But you are better than *boy*friend even. . . ."

"What do you mean?"

"You are *friend.* I have no friend before. Now I have friend."

"So have I," said Charlie.

"Next week you teach me American songs, *oui*?"

"Sure. Like what?"

"All kinds. Like 'South of the Border.' Is so beautiful tune. And also 'Star-Spangled Banner.' Is very hard song, 'Star-Spangled Banner.' "

"I know," said Charlie. "Even *I* can't sing it right. OK. I'll teach you it, and you can teach me *'La Marseillaise.'* "

Alan was just learning *"La Marseillaise,"* the French national anthem, in school.

"That is not song!"

"But it's the French national—"

"Dead!" the doll shrieked. "Is dead! I don't know dead songs! *She* knows. But *she* also is dead!" Naomi threw the doll to the floor. Then she leaped to the corner of her bed and crouched against the wall.

Alan felt his scalp become electric. He'd done it again! He'd said the wrong thing! What could he do? What could he *do*?

Alan took the doll and gingerly put it on the edge of the bed, in sitting position. Naomi didn't move.

"Hey, Yvette, kid," he made Charlie say to the doll. "I'm going to go to the library and get out a whole book of songs. OK? For you to read. OK, Yvette?"

Naomi's lips trembled as she tried to answer. She put her hand to her mouth.

"Yvette, kid? We're going to really have fun learning songs together. OK? . . . OK?"

With her hand over her mouth, in a faint voice, Naomi said for the doll, "Uh . . . uhkay."

"OK, I'll see you tomorrow, Yvette. *Au revoir*, kid. . . . Hey, aren't you going to say good-bye?"

Naomi crawled on the bed toward the doll, hesitated, then crawled over and snatched it to her. *"Au . . . Au revoir, Sharlee,"* she made it say, with a tremor still in her voice.

"Hey, that's supposed to be *Ch, Ch*, Charlie. Like that. Charlie."

"Ch?"

"That's right."

"*Char*-lie?" Naomi's doll-voice was less shaky now.

"Good!"

"Au revoir, Char-lie."

"Au revoir, Yvette."

Alan sighed with relief. Naomi wasn't frightened anymore. And as he made Charlie wave good-bye, Naomi made the doll wave back. He'd done something right, at last. He had hit a home run, for a change.

11

Alan put another library book on top of his growing pile. It was a book of Father Brown detective stories. Alan loved the stout little priest who solved mysteries with a twinkle in his eye.

He had taken three songbooks for Naomi, as well as a book on the history of baseball, a book of magic, and *The Call of the Wild*. But Alan wanted at least one Sherlock Holmes book. His eyes wandered along the shelves and down, from G. K. Chesterton to A. Conan Doyle. The only Sherlock Holmes book not out at the time was *The Hound of the Baskervilles*. The title chilled him. Alan had seen the movie, and it had been frightening from beginning to end. Maybe the book was good and scary, too. Alan added it to his pile.

The library always made Alan feel happy or angry or excited about the world. The titles alone were enough to pull him out of his body into other people's dreams and nightmares. *Dracula*. What a name! *The Count of Monte Cristo*. Swords like his father's razor, that could draw blood from a caress. *The Man in the Iron Mask*. Who could resist that? The titles were like drums calling you to a parade. Or a war. Or a hanging.

He carried the load of books to Mrs. Palumbo at the desk. Mrs. Palumbo and Alan had a special language of their own by now.

"Oh," said Mrs. Palumbo, "you're taking out books with red covers today, I see. I thought you had given up red covers."

"No, I need some red," said Alan. "For the hangar for my plane. I need a red hangar."

"Oh. All right. We have some nice red covers in our picture books. Would you like *The Three Bears*?"

"No, not *that* red."

"It's really more orange," said Mrs. Palumbo as she stamped the book cards, biting her lip to keep from laughing. "An orange-red. Like Goldilocks' hair."

"Well . . . I don't know. . . . I like my reds to be really red, you know? If I wanted a Goldilocks-colored hangar, that would be different."

"Of course," said Mrs. Palumbo. "It's a matter of taste. . . . Well, there you are, Alan, eight books. I think you've broken your own world's record."

"I need a lot of hangars. Thanks. Now I can give my mother her chopping board back. It's the wrong color."

At that, Mrs. Palumbo burst out laughing, but Alan forced himself to remain serious. It was understood, without saying it, that the one who laughed lost the game.

Alan carried the load of books home, shifting them to his left arm when his right arm started aching. When he reached his block, he pushed the thin, flat songbooks under his sweater, so the boys wouldn't see them. Books on magic and baseball were OK maybe, but *song*books!

"There goes the bookworm," called Carl Newman.

"Hey, look! He stole the whole library!" Joe Condello shouted.

Alan felt like shouting something back, but said nothing. His mind flashed to the time Joe had been reading a comic book and had asked Alan what the word "ruthless" meant. Alan had answered, "It's like you know, when a guy loses a girl named Ruth. Then he's ruthless." And Joe had believed it! Alan felt better as he hurried upstairs.

That evening Naomi met Alan in her living room for the first time. She seemed completely relaxed and cheerful. And when they went into her room, Alan noticed that there were no paper scraps anywhere. Good things were happening; it was like a Yankee winning streak. Alan decided the best thing to do was to just not think about it, or he might blow it, like a pitcher in a no-hit game.

When Naomi saw the songbooks, she made Yvette jump up and down.

"Oh, so many songs. Is *magnifique*! *Merci, Sharlee*," squeaked the doll. "You are *merveilleux, sans doute*."

"*Ch*arlie, it's pronounced."

"Char-lee."

Alan spread the books out on the bed. "Hey, look at *this* book," Charlie said. "*A Thousand and One Songs for Every Occasion*. Let's see. . . . There's a song for autumn. That's good; it's autumn now, almost. 'The Leaf Song.' Hmm . . . It looks lousy."

76

"Here is song for rainy day," said Yvette. "And next page, for sunny day. Is crazy book. *Peut-être*, they should have song for—how you call? *Ouragan?* . . . Hurricane! And song for earthquake."

"Earthquake, please don't shake," sang Charlie as Alan made up a song. "I have to bake a cake. Earthquake, stay away . . . uh . . . let me see. . . ."

"Earthquake, stay away." Yvette picked up the song. "We rather have big flood today."

"Here's 'The Star-Spangled Banner,' " said Charlie as Alan flipped through the pages of another book.

"Where is 'Over the Rainbow'?" asked Yvette.

"I can't find it. These songs are all old ones," Charlie answered. "Do you want to learn 'I've Been Working on the Railroad'?"

"*Non.* I like to learn 'Apple Tree—' "

"You mean 'Don't Sit Under the Apple Tree'?"

"*Ah oui.* And 'Praise Lord and Pass Ammunition.' And all songs on radio."

Alan was surprised. "Praise the Lord and Pass the Ammunition" was a war song. In a way, so was "Don't Sit Under the Apple Tree." She must not have connected them to the war in France. Did she think it was a different war? Just to be safe, Alan decided to teach her some other songs instead.

"Hey, I know a good one. You asked me about it last time. 'South of the Border.' OK? Let's start with that one. OK?"

"Uhkay."

In the next hour, through Charlie and Yvette, Alan

77

taught Naomi four new songs. She seemed to learn them perfectly after hearing them only a few times. Mrs. Liebman had been right; she *was* smart. But how could someone crazy be smart? Unless she wasn't really crazy at all? But if she wasn't really crazy, why had she sat tearing pieces of paper for two weeks?

Everything seemed confused to him. I'm actually having fun singing with her, he thought. All Shaun ever does when I sing is make dumb noises. I ought to do the same thing to him when he plays his harmonica.

"Ah Char-lee," said Yvette, as Alan started wrapping up the dummy at the end of the hour. "I have not really, really sang, so long time. Is like running, how you say . . . *nu-pieds* . . . no shoes? . . ."

"Barefoot?" asked Charlie.

"*Ah oui,*" Yvette answered. "Is like running barefooted in wet grass. Is so good."

She was right. That *was* how it felt. Shaun could never have said that. Even his mother couldn't have. And people thought she was crazy!

As she started making Yvette sing one of the songs again, Alan had the sudden thought that Naomi was his sister. Maybe the baby hadn't died. Maybe it was Naomi.

It was a crazy thought. Yet Alan felt he really had known Naomi somewhere, long ago. The eyes, the face, were so familiar. Where had he seen her before? It was in darkness. Somehow, he felt he'd seen her in the dark. But where?

12

In the following weeks, Alan sometimes felt that his Charlie McCarthy dummy was coming alive. And Yvette, the doll, seemed alive, too. At times he forgot he was doing the talking; he let Charlie say things that he, Alan, would never say. Charlie once called from his newspaper wrappings, "Hey, Yvette, babe, where are you, you gorgeous dish?"

And Yvette popped up from under the pillow. "Hello! *Je suis ici*, Charlie-dish!"

Yvette, that is, Naomi, was curious about everything, not just songs. What was a flat foot? What did "kick the bucket" mean? And "knock your block off"? So many words and phrases that Alan took for granted were totally confusing to her.

Alan made Charlie become a schoolteacher, with Yvette the one and only student in the class. A very mischievous student who would sometimes sneak away and hide under the pillow, or say "Cuckoo! Cuckoo! I am cuckoo clock and is time for lunch!"

Alan liked teaching Naomi-Yvette; it made him feel

like Mr. Danowitz, the science teacher, tall and calm and tremendously smart. But every day or so he had a sudden yearning to go out and run into the street with the boys and become part of the game. To sweat and spit, and curse when he missed a fly ball. To get slapped on the shoulder for a good hit. To make a perfect catch. To be with Shaun.

He couldn't wait for the weekends; then he could be himself both ways, with Shaun and with Naomi. He could run like a lunatic all day, then sit exhausted in Naomi's room and let Charlie and Yvette visit quietly. It had worked beautifully for several weekends.

One Saturday Shaun suggested flying the planes again, and they took the long walk up to Holmes. It felt good to be doing something just with Shaun; to get away from Joe Condello and Carl Newman and the others. Shaun was in his nutty mood; it was the Shaun Alan liked the best.

On the way to the airfield, Shaun stopped to help a discarded empty milk bottle cross the street, lifting it up and putting it down gently on the opposite curb.

"There you are, little bottle," Shaun said. "My good deed for the day. Not like Alan Silverman who doesn't care about bottles. Now run home to your mommy, little bottle."

The craziness continued all afternoon. At the airfield, Alan found a wooden spoon from an ice-cream Dixie cup. He scratched out a hole in the ground and buried the spoon.

"I want it to rest in peace," said Alan. "Dead spoons

80

can haunt you."

"You're nuts, Silverman," said Shaun. "Dead spoons go right to heaven."

"I don't care. I'm going to build a tomb for it, just like they did for Ulysses S. Grant." Alan piled stones around the spot and put a stick across the top. "There. Now let's see if we can find the spoon's wife."

The silliness went on and on. As they walked home, they pretended to fly the planes in their hands, like little kids, letting them rise and fall as if currents of air were pressing and releasing the wings. Alan really liked to "fly" his plane that way, making engine noises till his throat felt sore. But as they approached their block, Alan stopped the make-believe flight. Some of the boys might see him. Still, Shaun kept right on; he didn't seem to care.

As they rounded the corner, they saw that a stickball game was in progress.

"Hey!" called Shaun. "Can you guys use two more? One on each side."

"What do you know!" Joe Condello shouted. "The soapsuds twins are gonna separate!"

"We'll be down, soon as we put away the planes," Shaun called. "And we'll bring some soapsuds so you can wash behind the ears, Condello!"

Shaun was still "flying" his plane as they went into the lobby. They couldn't be seen now, so Alan started "flying" his plane again, pretending it was entering a gigantic cavern for secret meetings of the German high command. Hitler, Goebbels, Göring, the whole rotten bunch were in a secret conference aimed at smashing the Allied forces.

And Alan Silverman, in his Piper Cub, with his flying buddy, Madman Kelly, armed only with pistols and a couple of grenades, circled the huge cavern searching for the enemy. The assassination of Hitler was about to take place.

Then Alan stopped short. Coming down the stairs and into the lobby was Naomi, holding her doll. Good grief, thought Alan, she's too old to be carrying dolls around! She looks like a screwball. Her mother was just behind her, all in black, as if in mourning. They both look like nuts, thought Alan. Like complete nuts! He circled the lobby quickly with his plane, trying to get as far away as possible. In the lobby mirror, he saw that Naomi's mother was trying to lead her to the lobby door. But Naomi started walking toward Alan.

"Here comes Crazy Cat," whispered Shaun. "I wonder what's up. She always runs away from me."

Alan's mind churned as he hunted for excuses to cover anything she might say or do. Why couldn't she just go on out!

"Naomi, luz'm alain!" her mother called after her.

Alan understood that immediately. *Naomi, leave him alone!* It wasn't French; it was Yiddish. Alan's mother used Yiddish all the time, for emphasis, for sarcasm, for humor.

Yes, leave me alone, thought Alan. Damn!

But Naomi was right in front of him. She held up the doll and made it talk in the squeaky voice of Yvette.

"Charlie? Are you there?"

Alan looked at Shaun, trying to stall, not knowing what

to say. Shaun touched his head on the side with his finger, to indicate the girl was crazy. It certainly must seem insane to Shaun, thought Alan.

"Please, Charlie, visit me, today, *oui*? Charlie, please?"

"Oh yeah, sure, sure, anytime," said Alan as he slipped past Naomi and started "flying" his plane toward the stairway. Shaun followed, trying to race him.

He'd done the best he could, hadn't he? He *had* sort of said yes to her. But to Shaun it could sound as if he'd brushed aside a lunatic. What was wrong with that?

Then from the lobby, Naomi called up, "Charlie! You are friend. Please. *Please!*"

Alan felt himself bursting to call back down: Yes! Yes! I'm your friend! I'm always your friend, Naomi-Yvette!

But he couldn't. He couldn't. Why did everything you do, and everything you *didn't* do, always have to hurt?

13

Alan's father was studying his war map in the living room, checking it against the latest battlefront news in the evening paper. Alan headed straight for his bedroom, striding past his father without a glance, to make his message clear: *I don't want to talk about the war or anything. I want to be left alone!*

His father looked up and began to speak, but by then, Alan had slammed his bedroom door behind him. He leaped onto his bed and covered his head with his pillow.

What if she did that during a stickball game? He'd have to run away from her all the time, as if she had smallpox or something. Why did they have to pick *him* for this in the first place? Because he was "lovely"? That word made him punch the bed with his fist. For a split second he thought of what would happen if he threatened Naomi with the stickball bat when she came near him on the street. She'd leave him alone then! You bet she would! How was *that* for lovely!

The thought was horrible. How could you hate someone and like someone at the same time? He felt that way about his mother sometimes, and sometimes his father. But they were his parents; he knew he loved them, even though they could be gigantic pains in the neck. But he certainly didn't love Naomi. Who was she to him? No one. A crazy girl from upstairs, just as she was a month ago. . . . No, she wasn't. She was Naomi-Yvette now. She was his friend. They were each other's friends.

OK, they were friends. But how could he keep her from running over to him all the time? Maybe he should just explain to Mrs. Liebman that he and Naomi could only be friends indoors. Or maybe he could have Charlie tell Yvette that they should be secret friends. That wasn't bad, secret friends. Because secret friends don't show that they're friends outdoors or in apartment-house lobbies. Otherwise it wouldn't be a secret. That really might work. Everybody likes to have secret friends. He'd try it that evening. He'd *make* it work.

Someone was knocking gently on his bedroom door. Alan sat up, tossing the pillow aside. It was his father's knock. He might have been tapping on the door for a long time; the pillow had been over Alan's ears.

He suddenly remembered. The stickball game! He was supposed to play . . .

"Alan, can I talk with you?" his father asked from the other side of the door.

"I guess so."

His father came in and sat on the edge of the bed. "Are you all right?" he asked. "You looked pretty mad when you came in before."

"I'm OK."

"Good. Then I'll talk. . . . Your mother is afraid to ask you to do a certain something. She's afraid of your explosions."

"I don't explode!"

"What are you telling me? First your face turns red. Then you take some deep breaths. Then you explode. Like the Fourth of July. Don't worry about it; you've inherited your mother's temper, that's all. It's good. It's healthy. It's like an apple a day. It keeps the doctor away."

"What was the certain something she wanted me to do?"

"Oh yes, the something. Look, Alan, the girl you're helping upstairs, Naomi, she goes to a doctor. Once a week. And they discuss everything. How she's coming along. What should be done next. You know?"

"No . . . I mean, I didn't know."

"Anyway, they've discussed this business of your puppet talking to her doll. You know what I mean?"

"It's a *dummy*, not a puppet!"

"I apologize. I'm a dummy, when it comes to dummies. So they talked. And the doctor said you did a terrific job. You were able to become good friends with her using the dummy and the doll. She trusts you now. Terrific! The word 'terrific,' Mrs. Liebman told your mother, is exactly the word the doctor used. You can be proud. . . . What's the matter; you look worried. I said it was terrific."

"I'm worried about what comes *after* terrific." Alan felt a familiar sinking feeling inside.

"Alan, I couldn't have put it better myself. What comes

after terrific is this: she mustn't get too dependent on that doll. She can't use the doll as a crutch. You see?"

"But I thought it was supposed to be terrific."

"Absolutely. As a first step. But now she's got to take another step. And you have to help. You have to begin to talk to *her*. To Naomi Kirshenbaum. Direct."

"But I can't! She won't talk without the doll!"

"You have to try. You have to, as they say, wean her away from that doll. Yes?"

"Oh sure! I have to do everything! They ought to pay *me* instead of that nut doctor!"

"I don't like that, Alan. That's not *you* talking."

"Well I'm doing all the work!"

"That doctor is doing plenty of work. And in case you want to know, it's for free. And if the doctor says stop with the dummy, then you have to stop!"

"But she's scared stiff without that doll! I've tried it. It's impossible. . . ." Alan stood up and banged a desk drawer closed.

"Such a *tummel*! Such a noise! Your mother was right. It's the Fourth of July. . . . Listen, Alan, you don't understand. You do it slowly. Carefully. Not all of a sudden. Gently. A little bit. A little bit more. A touch. Another touch. You see?"

"OK, I'll do it," said Alan. "But if anything goes wrong, it'll be that doctor's fault, not mine!"

"That's fair enough."

"But it's not fair to her! Doesn't *she* count?"

"Of course. It's surgery, Alan. Sometimes you have to cut to cure. Things can't always be moonlight and roses.

When you had your appendix out, that wasn't moonlight and roses, right?"

"I'll say it wasn't."

"But now you can eat hot dogs, hamburgers, all kinds of *chozzerai*, and no more stomach aches. Alan, there's a real world. She has to be able to eat reality, so to speak. You follow me? Subways, schools, parks, friends, even enemies, everything. Life! You see?"

Alan sat on the bed again and thought for a moment. "I don't know," he said. "Maybe she's better off just with her doll."

"Alan, that's not life, that's death. The end of a person."

"All right! I *said* I'd do it! . . . But now how'll I explain about being secret friends?"

"What secret friends?"

"Well, I thought . . . oh, never mind."

14

On Monday, Alan made Charlie play with Yvette as he normally did for most of the visit. But toward the end, he made Charlie ask, "Hey, Yvette, kid. Did you know my real name is Charlie McCarthy Silverman? That's a pretty unusual name, huh?"

"*Oui*, is funny name. What is Silverman?"

"You know."

"*Non*. I don't."

Alan made the dummy point toward himself. "It's *his* name. Alan Silverman."

"He is gone. He is disappeared."

"Oh. . . . What's your name, Yvette? I mean your last name?" asked Charlie.

"Is just Yvette."

"But you must have a last name?"

"*Oui*. Is Yvette. My name is Yvette Yvette. And I have a middle name, too, which is still more Yvette. My name, complete, is Yvette Yvette Yvette. But my mother called me Simone. So at home, I was called Simone Yvette Yvette, but in school, Yvette Yvette Yvette. Is crazy, yes?"

Alan was tempted to make Charlie ask Yvette if her name was actually Yvette Yvette Kirshenbaum, but he decided it would be too sudden. Slowly, gently, his father had said.

"Well," asked Charlie, "where's your mother then?"

"My mother is gone. Disappeared."

"But who was she when she was here?"

"Ah. *Her*," said Yvette, as Naomi made the doll gesture toward herself. "But she's gone."

"Then who are the people in this room?"

"*Us!* We are here, Charlie," said Yvette.

It was no use. She managed to find answers every time. If Naomi wasn't there, then there was no way of talking to her. He gave up for that afternoon.

Before going to bed that night, Alan wondered how he could make Naomi look at him, really see him, rather than Charlie. If he left Charlie behind, Yvette probably wouldn't talk at all.

Alan searched through his closet full of old toys, looking for an idea. He'd been through his toys and games a dozen times by now, searching for new things to do with Naomi-Yvette. He was tired of the whole mess of broken and discarded objects. Then Alan saw his battered magician's top hat, and his thoughts took a jump. He would dress nuttily, and force her to see him! Now where was that false mustache that had come with the hat?

He pushed things around in his closet for half an hour, until he finally discovered the remains of the black mustache camouflaged in the box of black dominoes. He tried on the mustache and the hat. Not bad. He'd be a hobo magician, and Charlie could be his assistant. She'd have to notice him now.

That next evening, Alan put on his hat and mustache before going into Naomi's apartment. Mrs. Liebman smiled as she led Alan to Naomi's room.

"It's not yet Halloween, Alan. But still, I'll give you a treat instead of a trick." She handed Alan another of her endless candy bars.

"Thank you, but I don't like it with nuts," said Alan, handing the chocolate bar back. He wished she would stop acting as if she had to pay him all the time. He was beginning to wonder if Mrs. Liebman was really as nice as his mother thought she was.

Naomi was lying on her bed reading a book with a title in French. Alan felt silly with his mustache and dummy. She seemed so normal, so intelligent, lying there reading that book.

Naomi looked up from the book, and fought back a smile as she stared at Alan's mustache. Then she grabbed Yvette and held the doll up.

"Charlie, come out, please," called Yvette.

"Get ready for the magic show," answered Charlie. "I'm the assistant. He's the magician."

"Ah no. I hate magic," said Yvette. "Is only make-believe. I rather I sing with you, Charlie, uhkay?"

And though he tried several times, Alan couldn't get Naomi-Yvette to watch any tricks. She'd found a way to avoid seeing Alan as Alan, again.

By Thursday, Alan was convinced that she would never let go of Yvette and Charlie. When he told his father how impossible it was, his father said that in a way it showed the doctor was right. If it were easy, it wouldn't have mattered so much. Keep trying. Keep trying.

OK. He'd keep trying. But it was hopeless.

On Friday, Alan had a new idea. Charlie and Yvette had continued to play school every so often. Today, Alan decided to make *himself* part of the school. He would be Mr. Boomladle, the principal, visiting the class.

"Now class, Mr. Boomladle is here," Alan made Charlie say. "Yvette, would you tell Mr. Boomladle what you learned about Abraham Lincoln."

"He freed all slaves," said Yvette. But the doll was made to speak, not to Alan, but toward the wall behind Charlie.

"*I* am Mr. Boomladle," said Alan, in a deep voice. "Speak directly to me, please."

"But Boomladle is there!" said Yvette. Naomi made the doll point above Charlie's head. "He is big fat man with red nose."

"If that's Boomladle," said Charlie, "then who's *he*?" Charlie gestured toward Alan.

"Is blackboard," said Yvette with great assurance.

Hopeless! Just plain hopeless! What was left? What could he do? . . . The secret friends. Maybe she'd feel safe talking about being secret friends.

"Hey, Yvette, kid. Let's quit playing school," said Charlie. "Let's be serious, OK?"

"Uhkay."

"Yvette, kid," said Charlie, "I'm your friend, right?"

"Ah oui."

"And you're *my* friend," said Charlie. "We're friends all the time. Even when I'm in *his* closet, and when you're in *her*—wherever she keeps you—"

"I sleep in big dresser drawer," said Yvette. "Stupid place."

"But we're always secret friends, right?"

"Certainement."

"But we shouldn't let anyone else know. It's no fun that way. We shouldn't ever talk out in the street," said the dummy to the doll. "Or in the lobby or the hallway. Nowhere, except here. That's the way to be secret friends, OK?"

"Uhkay."

"Hey, that's terrific!"

So far, so good. The dummy and the doll were secret friends. Now for the next step. This was it. No more Boomladles. No more Charlies. Alan to Naomi, straight. That's what they wanted. That's what they were going to get. A week was enough.

"And how about *you* being *my* secret friend, too, Naomi?" Alan asked in his normal voice. "I'd like to be *your* secret friend."

"Charlie," said Yvette, in her squeaky voice, "Charlie, we are secret friends, uhkay?"

"Naomi, I want you to be my secret friend, too. My name is Alan."

"NON! NON!" Naomi grabbed the Charlie McCarthy dummy from Alan and hurled it against the wall. The dummy's head, which had been loose before, crashed across the room, free from the body.

"NON!" Naomi fell flat on the floor and pushed herself under the bed. Mrs. Liebman and Mrs. Kirshenbaum rushed to the bedroom door, but Alan didn't notice.

His thoughts were full of static, like a radio gone wild. Quick! You stupid jerk! Do something! Now! Quick! Charlie! Get Charlie!

He grabbed the dummy's head from under the dresser, pushed it against the body, and started to make Charlie talk to Yvette.

"Hey, Yvette, kid! Yvette, kid! Look! I'm OK! This is Charlie talking. Charlie. I'm OK. They can fix me up. Look. Yvette, look!"

There was a silence in the room. Alan looked under the bed. Naomi was crouched against the wall, both fists up against her face. They'd better get that doctor, he thought. They better get someone. What could he *do*?

Give the doll to her! Alan took the doll and slid it toward Naomi. She slammed it with one arm and the doll hurtled against the opposite wall.

Do something else! Anything! Make Charlie talk to Naomi. Try it!

"Hey, it's me. Charlie McCarthy. I'm Yvette's friend. And I'm *your* friend, too. Come on out . . . Naomi, kid."

"MERDE!" Naomi screamed. *"MERDE! MERDE!"*
Don't stop! Try once more.

"Come on, Naomi. Come on out," Alan said gently, in his own voice.

Mrs. Liebman touched Alan on his shoulder. "Ssh, Alan. Good enough for today. Come. She'll be all right. Come."

94

"In a minute," said Alan. It wasn't good enough, at all. It was miserable.

He whispered to Naomi, "*Au revoir. Au revoir*, Naomi, kid. I'm your friend. Can't you just say *au revoir* to me, Naomi?"

There was a long silence under the bed. Then there was a slight stirring, and Naomi said, in Yvette's voice, "She is dead. . . . She is dead . . . dead. . . ."

Alan looked toward Mrs. Liebman and Mrs. Kirshenbaum for some answer or some help.

"It's all right, Alan," said Mrs. Liebman. "It's all right. Please come back to visit, soon. . . . Yes? Please?"

But it wasn't all right! It wasn't! His thoughts swarmed like angry bees. I messed it up! Clumsy, stupid jerk! I did it! Everything I do! Everything I say! She's worse than ever! I did it! Now she doesn't even have Yvette! And I did it!

15

Alan realized that sometime that night they must have had a meeting. A secret meeting. They. His parents, Mrs. Liebman, Mr. Liebman, maybe Mrs. Kirshenbaum, possibly even the doctor. Alan wondered if all of New York City had had a meeting while he was asleep.

"A day off, Alan," his mother had said the next morning. "For you. For her. We decided it's better to give it a day's rest. Go to the Saturday matinee with the boys; my treat. Buy some ice cream, popcorn, anything you want. I'll even treat your friend, the Kelly boy. Go. Enjoy. . . . Please, Alan, stop looking like that."

"I loused the whole thing up!"

"Go to the movies and forget. If I acted like you every time every little thing went wrong, I'd be already in the crazy house. It's an Abbott and Costello movie. Go already!"

"But it's not a little thing—"

"Alan! You're driving me *meshugge*! Go!"

The movie theater smelled of old musty carpeting as

always. The silken layers of curtains covering the screen glowed pink, blue, green. The colors seemed to blend as the curtains stirred.

Alan usually enjoyed this part of the matinee, the lights up and everyone fooling around as they waited for the show to begin. He liked to come early, when the doors opened, just for this. But today, it felt almost mean to sit there while Naomi was—what? He pictured her sulking in a corner, tearing up pieces of paper again. Afraid to take a breath. . . . He had to forget about her. He just had to! Alan stared at the glowing curtain, trying to see if he could hypnotize himself.

"Hey, this is the life, Alan," Shaun said, putting his feet over the seat in front. "My mother never treated *you* to anything. How come your mother's treating me? She doesn't even like me."

"I guess she hit her head on a frying pan or something. Who can figure out mothers, right?"

More boys joined them, boys they knew from school or the block, and soon there were eleven of them in one row. One of the boys started calling, "We want the show! We want the show!" and in a few seconds the entire row was doing it, clapping their hands in rhythm.

The usher came down and aimed his flashlight directly at Alan's face.

"If you guys don't stop it, OUT!"

"Boo hoo," said Shaun, as Alan nudged him to be quiet.

"Get your feet off that seat, you little creep!"

"Oh yes, sir," said Shaun, moving his feet down. "I'm

sorry, sir. Please forgive me, sir. I'll be a good little boy, sir."

The usher stared at him viciously for a minute, then left.

"Swallow your flashlight, sir, and light it, and you can turn yourself into a jack-o'-lantern, sir," Shaun whispered to the boys. The entire row roared with laughter. The usher hesitated, came down a few paces, thought better of it, and retreated.

A group of girls from Alan's junior high school class came down the aisle, spotted Alan, Shaun, and the others, and moved into the row right in front of them.

"Oh no," said Shaun. "They'll spoil the whole movie."

"Hey look," said one of the boys. "The sewing class has arrived. Oink, oink, oink, oink."

A few of the girls laughed, but none of them turned around.

Another boy took the long flowing hair of the girl in front of him and started carefully lifting her hair up, slowly, so she couldn't feel it. The others watched intently.

Suddenly, the girl, Gloria Carmella, swirled around. "You cut that out, Robert J. Fehling, Junior, or I'll call the usher!"

All the girls turned around now.

"I was just trying to see if you had a head attached to all that hair, that's all, Gloria J. Carmella, *Junior*. If you don't like it, why don't you move?"

"It's a free country. We can sit anywhere we want," said Gloria.

"Then why don't you sit on my lap?" Robert asked.

The boys laughed, and three or four of the girls laughed, too.

"You're the freshest and stupidest person in this—in this whole movie theater!" said Gloria. "I'm not going to pay any attention to you! You can't bother me, 'cause I won't let you."

"OK. Then I'll sit on *your* lap. I'm climbing over the seat." Robert made a motion to climb, and Gloria gave a tiny shriek. There was more laughter as Gloria's face turned red. Then she suddenly started laughing, too. She turned her head back toward Robert again. "You're terrible! I hate you!" Then she turned back.

Alan liked the way her hair swirled as she turned back and forth. He wished he could touch her hair for a moment, the way Robert had.

He thought of Naomi again. He tried to imagine her sitting there with the other girls, having fun. But he couldn't. She'd have to sit there with a doll; she'd have to talk with Yvette. She'd look crazy. She *was* crazy.

His father was right! The doctor was right! Seeing these girls made it absolutely clear. She had to give up that doll. She had to become . . . a girl! Herself! Naomi! For a second he pretended she was sitting in front of him, and he touched her hair, and she turned and said . . . What would she have said? Would she have been angry? Maybe she would have smiled. Just smiled. That's what she would have done; she would have smiled. Naomi get better now, quick, he thought. Get better.

"Cut it out, Ralph!" another girl called out. "Ralph pushed his foot between the seat! He did!"

"Tell his mommy," said one of the boys.

Shaun nudged Alan. "Come on! They're just one big pain. Let's move to the back! We won't be able to watch the show."

Alan wanted to stay. During the movie, some of the boys would make remarks about the picture which made everything seem silly or crazy up on the screen. And sometimes they made the actors' words sound like a dirty joke. The girls giggled, though half the time the jokes didn't make any sense. It was fun. It really was fun. Why was Shaun such a sourpuss?

"Come on, Alan, let's go. Those girls are crazy. We won't hear anything."

Reluctantly, Alan moved to a back row with Shaun. But he promised himself that next time he'd go to a matinee by himself.

The lights dimmed, and the show started with a series of Bugs Bunny cartoons. Alan sank back in his seat, loaded his mouth with cherry-flavored chocolates, and let himself float.

The cartoons were followed by a Shadow serial, then a Three Stooges comedy short. Then the newsreel came on. The Battle of Leyte in the Pacific. Landing boats, destroyers, aircraft overhead. Soldiers fighting on the beaches. Then the war in Europe. V-bombs hitting London, whole blocks of houses blazing. Men with soot-blackened faces, holding huge fire hoses, fighting a wall of fire. Bodies in the street. A child, half-bent, arm twisted out of shape, dead.

No one was laughing now.

Adolf Hitler, briefly, shown walking with his officers. The theater filling with boos, loud, loud against the hated man.

Then General Eisenhower with U.S. troops, and the theater shaking with shouts and cheers. And Alan shouting, too, shouting because the others were shouting, shouting for his mother and father who hated Hitler so much, shouting for himself, for Naomi, for her mother, for the Liebmans, for everyone!

And then, the Abbott and Costello comedy. The real movie had begun, and Alan curled up and let himself float away again. It felt good to not have to be Alan Silverman for a while. To not have to be anyone at all.

16

Sunday breakfast had always been Alan's favorite meal of the week. His father would buy fresh rolls from the bakery, and bring home the newspapers. Then, while Alan read the comics on the living-room carpet, from back to front to save *Dick Tracy* for last, his father took over the kitchen.

This morning, Alan's father was making his specialty: eggs scrambled with chopped onions and mushrooms. No one could make scrambled eggs like his father; they came out exactly right, fluffy to perfection.

Alan could tell by the sound of the fork stirring in the pan that the eggs were almost ready. The shrill scratching from the kitchen was becoming thicker and duller. Hitler, the war, all the terrors of yesterday's newsreel seemed very far away. The carpet with its worn curving patterns that he had once made into highways for his toy cars, this carpet was far more real. The war was a fairy tale, almost.

Almost . . . except for Naomi. She'd been there; she'd been in it. The Nazis had taken over her country. Had driven her crazy. If only she could be like those girls at the movie, he thought. If she could just forget about the war and the Nazis and everything. She could be here with me, right now, reading the comics. She could even have breakfast with us. She could almost be a part of the family.

Alan turned toward his mother. She was reading the paper and drinking her first coffee of the day from her favorite cup, the one with the chipped rim.

"Mom, could you and Dad ever adopt Naomi?"

"That's a question."

"Huh? Why couldn't you?"

"She *has* a mother. What does she need, two mothers?"

"Well, she doesn't have a father. And you always wanted to have a—" Alan stopped short, not finishing the word "daughter." But his mother had filled in the blank. She looked as if she were about to cry. Then she suddenly called toward the kitchen, "Sol, are you cooking those eggs, or hatching them?"

His father's voice came back, "Another minute. No rushing. Masterpieces can't be rushed."

"Anyway, Naomi could use a super-duper mother and father like you and Dad," said Alan, trying to be extra cheerful.

"What's so super-duper?"

"I don't know. You're a terrific Monopoly player."

"*Oy!* Write that on my gravestone, please."

"*And* you're a pretty not-bad cook. I mean, like your split-pea soup, alone, is worth having you as a mother for."

"Sol!" she called to the kitchen. "You should hear this!"

103

"And Dad's scrambled eggs, too. That's worth having him as a father for."

His mother laughed. "Alan, sometimes you can be a pain in the *tochis*, and sometimes you can be the funniest, loveliest—"

"MOM!"

"Not lovely. Not lovely. I'm sorry. Not lovely."

His father called from the kitchen, "Come and get it!"

"Mom," Alan said hurriedly as they went to the kitchen, "do you think, if Naomi gets better, she could come down here and have breakfast with us, and all, sometime?"

"Why not? As a matter of fact, she's coming down here after breakfast today. I didn't tell you?"

"No."

"She's coming. We have a half hour or so before we have to go to your Aunt Sarah. She's coming down for a very short visit. We thought it's good to get her out of her room. Yes?"

Alan sat down at the kitchen table with a heavy thud. "You always decide things without me. How come? Don't I get to know anything till the last second?"

"You were asleep when we talked with the Liebmans last night," Alan's father said as he filled their plates with scrambled eggs.

"You're always having secret conferences!"

"Listen, I work hard, like a nobody, five days a week. Let me have a secret conference once in a while. It makes me feel like a big shot. Like Roosevelt and Churchill."

"It's not funny!"

"Alan, you're right," said his father. "When you're right, you're right. Next time we'll talk to you ahead of time. Now eat my masterpiece before it gets cold and becomes a lump of library paste."

The breakfast was truly splendid. His father had opened some strawberry jam for the rolls, and that was the final luxury. Alan even nibbled at the crumbs, after the roll was gone.

Shortly after breakfast, the doorbell rang.

"Alan, you go," said his father. "With us, she might be scared. So listen, be careful, you know, and very easy with her, yes? We'll be in our room. In case of emergency, you call us, right?"

His father had made things sound serious. Alan felt a sudden helplessness. What should he say to her? "Hello, Naomi"? "Hi, kid"? . . . What?

Alan went to the door, trying out different ways of saying hello. But when he opened the door, only Mrs. Liebman was there.

"Good morning, Alan," she said. Then she turned toward the stairway and called, "Naomi, come. Your friend is here. Come. . . ."

Slowly, sadly, Naomi came down the stairs. In her hand was a torn piece of paper. But no Yvette!

"There we are. See. We're all good friends this morning. Alan is going to show you his house, and his games, and everything, yes, Alan? Come, Naomeleh. Come." Mrs. Liebman led Naomi past the door, then waited to make sure she didn't turn and run.

Alan made way for Naomi. She walked past him, head

down, into the living room. Then she looked up slowly, and stared at herself in a large mirror on the wall. Alan didn't know what to say, so he just walked over to Naomi and stood next to her, looking in the mirror. Then he raised his hand and waved.

"Hello," said Alan, but his voice sounded hollow to him.

Naomi continued to stare at the mirror. Her fear made the room around them seem cold and unfriendly, like the waiting room at the doctor's office.

"Who's that?" asked Alan, pointing at his reflection in the mirror. There was a long silence. Then Alan decided to answer his own question. "That's me. Alan Silverman. Also known as A. A. Boomladle."

"Charlie?" said Naomi very softly.

"Charlie's in the hospital getting fixed up."

Naomi sat down abruptly on the carpet and started tearing the paper in her hand.

"Hey, Naomi, kid. *Comment allez-vous*, huh? How are things?"

Naomi shifted her position to face away from Alan. She had torn all the paper, but she picked up the scraps and started tearing them into smaller and smaller pieces. Alan hated those scraps of paper. He had to get her attention, somehow.

"*Comment allez-vous, Naomi?* . . . I'll count to ten. If you don't answer by ten, I'm going to, uh . . . *cry!* That's it! I'm going to cry. *Un . . . deux . . . trois . . . quatre . . .*"

Alan had a thought. He'd pretend he didn't know the

next number. That might do it.

"Uh . . . Let me see. . . . *Un, deux, trois, quatre* . . . uh . . ."

"Cinq!" said Naomi in a sudden burst. Good! He wasn't messing things up. Careful. Careful. Again . . .

"Cinq, six, sept . . . uh . . . *sept* . . . Wait a minute. . . . *Cinq, six, sept* . . . Oh boy . . . *sept* . . ."

"Stupid! *Huit!*"

It was working! It was *her* voice! Naomi Kirshenbaum's voice! No high squeaky doll's voice! Hers!

"Huit? It can't be," said Alan. "Wheat is what you eat. How can that be a number? You're wrong."

"Fou!"

"Oh *fou!* Right! *Un, deux, trois, quatre, cinq, six, sept, fou, neuf, dix.* Now I'm gonna cry."

He had counted: one, two, three, four, five, six, seven, *fool*, nine, ten. Was that a slight smile on Naomi's face?

"Comment allez-vous? Answer me now, or I'll really cry. And boys don't cry." said Alan. "Never."

Naomi shrugged. She studied the scraps of paper in her hand. Then she dropped all the scraps on the floor and shrugged again. She looked at Alan for a moment, then said, in her normal voice, *"Ah oui.* And girls don't sneeze . . . ever."

Alan stared directly into Naomi's eyes and saw the twinkle of mischief there, the intelligence, the imagination that had been Yvette. Naomi turned and looked around the room. Then she stood up and studied herself in the mirror again. Alan stood next to her.

"Hello, Naomi," he said, looking at her in the mirror.

She stood quietly looking back at Alan. Then her mouth opened and closed as if she were speaking, but Alan heard nothing.

"Do you like my house?" he asked toward the mirror.

Naomi turned away and walked slowly around the living room, touching the top of the table, the sofa, the lamp. Then she stopped in front of a group of framed photographs. Three or four were of Alan; others were of his grandmother, his father and mother, and his cousins. She touched each photograph, then picked up one of Alan and stared at it.

"That's me, two years ago," said Alan.

"Is nice house," she said, answering his earlier question. She put down the photo and walked around the room once more. Then she studied the photographs again.

Alan's mother appeared at the far end of the living room.

"We'll have to start going to Aunt Sarah now. Maybe you take Naomi back upstairs now, Alan, all right?" Then she raised her hand, while Naomi was looking at the photographs, and made the V-for-Victory sign that Churchill used in Great Britain.

And it *was* a victory, there was no doubt about it. But what had he done, Alan wondered. Nothing. Absolutely nothing. But he made a V-sign with his fingers, back toward his mother, just to keep her happy. If she wanted to think he was a hero or something, why argue? "Hero" was a lot better than "lovely."

17

Alan's Aunt Sarah and Uncle Phil lived in a large old apartment in Manhattan, a few blocks west of Central Park. The living room seemed musty to Alan, as if it needed air and sun, and people shouting or laughing. Alan's cousins were both in the Navy, fighting somewhere in the Pacific, and his aunt and uncle had closed their apartment like a book because their sons were gone.

Alan remembered the Battle of Leyte he'd seen in the newsreel, and wondered if his cousins had been there. No one knew. All through dinner the talk was about the war in the Pacific. Again and again, his uncle and aunt came back to their worries about their sons in battle.

"What can you do?" his uncle said. "Every day, I thank God we have no telegrams. That's all."

A telegram could mean that one of his cousins had been wounded, or worse, killed in action.

It was painful to sit there, and after dinner Alan asked if he could go for a long walk in the park.

"Go, Alan," his father said. "Enough war headaches. Enjoy. But be back by five."

"And don't get lost," his mother added.

"Mom! I know my way around Central Park! We've been there a million times!"

"But not by yourself," his mother said. "So stop the mouth!"

"OK, OK," said Alan as he retreated toward the door.

"Alan," his Aunt Sarah said, "a mother worries, whether her sons are fighting in the war or running around Central Park. That's what a mother is for, no?"

"And a father," his uncle added.

"OK, OK, OK," said Alan.

When he reached the park, Alan decided to walk toward the big lake, the Rowboat Lake as he called it. His father had taken him rowing there many times. He slowed his pace at a series of little bridges and twisting paths that looped under and over one another near the north end of the lake. It was one of his favorite spots. He imagined Indians hiding behind a high, rocky formation, just as he always had imagined in this place. . . . But there hadn't been any Indians here for three hundred years, and he was too old for make-believe Indians. It was dumb, he told himself.

Alan walked along the edge of the lake, past the boathouse, past the Bethesda Fountain, up to the mall with its long expanse of lawns and its double row of benches and statues. He'd often walked on the benches for the whole length of the mall, stepping from bench to bench, hopping off only to avoid people sitting in the way. The park was almost empty now, and the benches ahead formed a long, straight "railway track." It was tempting.

If Shaun were with him, maybe he would do it. Or Naomi. But alone, he was too old. It was strange. He felt older when he was alone.

The scattered people sitting on the benches looked lonely. Maybe the ones who had other people to be with were having dinner. And the rest never ate.

Alan sat on one of the benches in the mall. Now that he'd stopped walking and had no destination, he felt as lonely as the others must have felt. He had become one of them. He was just another gray person, sitting on a bench, alone, in this big mall full of statues.

She always seemed so lonely. Naomi. In the hallway. On her bed. Even in his living room. Everywhere. She was always so lonely. Maybe it felt like this to her. His feeling now. Being completely alone. Maybe, to her, he was a statue that had talked. A statue that had un-aloned her. A friendly statue. Something like that. Maybe.

He imagined Naomi next to him, and challenged her to a race along the benches. *Uhkay*. Then he got up and ran the length of the mall on the benches, but not so fast as to beat her. A tie, he thought to himself. Good race, Naomi! Good race!

It was crazy. He wondered if Naomi ever imagined things like that about him. Probably not. . . . Still, it would be sort of nice if she actually did. Would he ever know? Probably not. . . . But, somehow, he felt less lonely now. It was crazy.

18

On Monday evening, Naomi came downstairs with Mrs. Liebman again.

"Hi, Naomi, kid," said Alan at the door.

Naomi shrugged, then walked past Alan into the living room. She circled the room as she'd done the day before, touching everything again, as if for luck.

"Hey. How are you, Naomi?" Alan asked.

"Charlie, are you there?"

"No. Charlie isn't here. I'm here, though. You know, Alan? Me? . . . Hi."

Naomi walked around slowly, then said, "I like your house."

"It's pretty good. I mean it's not great, but it's OK. We're not rich, you know? But it's OK. . . . My mother keeps cleaning everything all the time. So it looks better than it is, you know? . . . Hey, would you like to see my room?"

"Yes, I think."

Good, thought Alan. Good.

"Come on. I'll show you all my stuff. It's at the end of the hall there."

Naomi sat stiffly on Alan's bed while he showed her his airplanes, his games, all the broken toys in his closet. Every so often Naomi said, "Is nice," but she seemed lost and afraid. What was he doing wrong, Alan wondered. Maybe she wanted to look at the things herself, as she'd done in the living room yesterday.

"Hey, I'll tell you what. I'll be back in a couple of minutes, OK? Play with anything you want. Go ahead. I'll be back." Alan left the room, and watched from the hall.

Naomi remained on the bed, stroking the cover. Then she stood up and walked around the room touching things, as she'd done in the living room. She stopped at Alan's Spitfire model hanging by a string from the ceiling. She nudged it gently, and the plane turned. She ducked her head under it to watch it swing.

Good! I've done something right again, Alan thought. She really likes my plane. She's kind of actually playing with it. I did the right thing. And I did it by myself!

Then to Alan's amazement, Naomi said out loud the one word, "Spitfire." She knew what it was! And she wasn't a bit afraid of it, even though it was a pursuit plane used in the war. Only certain things seemed to bother her. Naomi pushed the plane again, gently.

Alan went back into his room. "Do you like my model?"

"Is nice."

"You can have it if you want."

"Oh, *non*. Is too nice. No, I cannot. Th-thank you. . . ."

"I mean it. You can have it."

She was stuttering and seemed very tense. She bit her fingernail for a moment. Then she spoke again.

"Thank you . . . Ch- . . . Ch- . . . Th- . . . thank you A- . . . Alan."

HIS NAME! She had never said his name. She had almost said "Charlie" just then. Why was it so hard for her to say his name? Never mind. She'd said it. It had to be good! It was good!

"You're welcome, Naomi. If you ever want my Spitfire, it's yours. OK?"

"Uhkay."

Naomi sat stiffly on the bed again, pushing some checkers on an old checkerboard from Alan's closet.

"You want to play checkers, Naomi?"

"Uhkay."

Alan set up the board, and turned the red checkers toward Naomi.

"You move first."

They played in silence, but Alan noticed that Naomi thought very carefully before each move. And her moves were clever. The game ended in a draw.

Mrs. Liebman had come back down for Naomi. As Naomi walked to the front door, she turned back toward Alan and gave a little wave, opening and closing her hand in precisely the same way that Alan had waved to her in the mirror yesterday. Then she smiled. The smile he'd imagined at the movie! That exact same smile!

The thought rose in him like the rise of breakers coming toward him when he swam at the shore. I like Naomi Kirshenbaum. The thought rose and fell again, like the pull up and down of the sea. I like her. . . . I like her. I really do . . . I like her.

19

For the next several days, Naomi hardly spoke during her visits to Alan. She touched things in the room in a repeating ritual, though Alan noticed she touched fewer objects each evening. He had counted twelve items on Tuesday, eight on Wednesday, but only three on Thursday: his desk, his lamp, and the Spitfire.

Naomi seemed content to do whatever Alan suggested. On Tuesday, Alan taught her how to play Monopoly. But Naomi spoke just enough to play the game and no more. Still, she did call him Alan now, with a little twist of accent that made the name Alan tinkle like a bell. Alan liked his name when she said it that way. It became special.

"I am landed on jail, Alan," she would say. Or "Alan, I build a house on, how you pronounce it, Penn-syl-vania Avenue."

But Naomi was quiet and even a little stiff until, in the middle of a checker game on Thursday, she finally forgot herself completely. Alan had jumped three of her checkers in a row.

Naomi clapped her hands in admiration.

"Hey, don't you want to win?" asked Alan.

"*Ah oui. Ah oui.* But it was so nice. Boom, boom, *boom*! Is beautiful."

"You're a good sport, Naomi, kid."

"Sport? What is a good sport? Is checkers, yes?" She was asking questions again, as she had done with Yvette.

"No, it's like . . . a good sport is a person who sort of doesn't really care if he loses. Like you. That's a good sport."

"The person, *they* are the sport?"

"Right. There's a lot of meanings. Baseball is a sport, OK? But someone who spends a lot of money on you is called a sport. And a good loser is a good sport. But checkers isn't a sport, it's a game. OK, Naomi, sport?"

"Uhkay," said Naomi, "I try to remember, Alan. But English language is crazy, *oui*?"

That next morning in homeroom, Mrs. Landley asked Alan to see her after school. What was wrong now, Alan wondered. What had he done? The butterfly bombardment? Was she bothered about that after all these weeks?

Alan turned and looked at Shaun across the room. Shaun gave an enormous shrug to make clear he didn't know what was the matter.

At the end of the day, Alan walked back to Mrs. Landley's room with Shaun.

"You can go home, Shaun. I can take care of myself," said Alan.

"Naah. You're too scared, baby boy. You need help. Look, your knees are shaking."

"I am *not* scared! And quit calling me baby boy!"

"OK, baby boy. Anyway, I'd like to see what happens. It's a free show."

"What if I don't want you to see what happens?"

"That's you," said Shaun. "Secret Silverman. Everything always has to be a big secret."

"What? I don't have any secrets!"

"How about that secret errand of yours? . . . Hey, are you ever going to tell me about it? I'm supposed to be your friend."

"I . . . I just can't, that's all," said Alan. Could he? He'd asked himself many times. That day at Holmes he almost had.

"OK," said Shaun. "But if I had some kind of secret, I'd tell *you*. You know I would."

"Well . . . Look, you can come with me to Mrs. Landley's room," said Alan. "OK?"

"Oh, thanks a lot. . . . OK. Great! I hope she smacks you with a yardstick. Right on your rear end."

"You're crazy."

"Hi-ho, Silverman!"

"Cut it out, Shaun!"

"Away!"

Mrs. Landley was seated at her desk marking test papers. Alan and Shaun took a few steps into the classroom, then waited. The empty classroom seemed forbidding; after three P.M., it wasn't their special home any longer. It was Mrs. Landley's.

"Oh, boys, hello! My goodness, the day has flown," said Mrs. Landley, pushing the test papers to the side.

118

"You did very well, Shaun. Ninety-five; very nice paper; but you must learn how to spell 'occur.' And Alan, really, try not to say 'sort of' in an essay. 'He was sort of . . .' what was it you wrote?"

She thumbed through the papers. "Oh, yes. Here it is. 'He was sort of short compared to the other players on the team.' Try 'rather short' or 'fairly short' or just plain 'short compared to' et cetera, et cetera, et cetera. You've gotten a ninety-six, very nice, but your handwriting is disgraceful. Now, what did I want to see you about?"

"You wanted to break a yardstick over his head," said Shaun.

"Please, Shaun Kelly. I'm at my nerves' end by this time of day. I hope you never become a teacher. Avoid it. Avoid it like the plague. Now let me see. . . . Yes! Alan! I remember! . . . Shaun, I'm sorry, but I'd like to speak to Alan, alone. Would you mind?"

It sounded serious. What could it be? Alan felt sweat under his arms.

"OK. So long, Silverman. See you at your funeral," Shaun said as he headed for the door.

"Thanks," said Alan.

When Shaun was gone, Mrs. Landley took some textbooks from the side closet and stacked them on her desk. Alan could tell at a glance that the set of books matched his own.

"There! Alan, these books are for a friend of yours. Naomi—how do you pronounce her last name?"

Alan blew out a long breath of relief. "Kirshenbaum," he said.

"Yes, of course. Poor girl. What a terrible story. I understand you've been helping her a great deal. You can feel quite proud of yourself. Of course, I know you by now, and perhaps you don't feel proud at all. You have so much insight for your age, perhaps you just feel lucky to have what it takes to help, you see."

Lucky? Alan's mind juggled with the word. His father had said that, too. *Was* he lucky? And *did* he have what it takes? If he did, why was he still hiding Naomi from Shaun and all the others? And why was he so glad that Shaun had left and couldn't hear all this?

"Alan, are you listening?"

"Uh huh."

"You don't like praise, do you?"

"Uh uh."

"No, I suppose not. I don't blame you. Adults are such pains in the neck. So condescending. They think children are children. And they aren't; that's the secret. Sometimes, I forget. . . . Well, Alan, here are Naomi's books. We hope the day will arrive when she'll be joining us. She's very bright. She belongs in the Rapid Advance class, in spite of the usual American history and grammar problems. But others from Europe did it; she can, too. There's Rudolph Steinman in 8A-R; he's done very well. So we hope you'll help her. I know you will."

"But what do I *do*? I don't know what she should read."

"We've given a series of study guides to Mrs. . . . I've forgotten her name."

"Mrs. Liebman?"

"That's the person. She has study guides and she'll have

120

weekly lesson plans. But we had to gather these books. And you *are* strong; you can carry two loads of books home easily. . . . So your job is just to help her over the rough spots. Try to give her some of the flavor of our classroom discussions. Including butterflies, where needed. By the way, some unnamed teachers might have placed you on suspension for that, Alan. . . ."

She *hadn't* really liked it! He'd thought not, even then!

"Why didn't *you*?" asked Alan, swallowing the words.

"Because I'm not some unnamed teachers. And besides, I think you're great."

"That's OK," said Alan. "I sort of think you're great, too."

"Ah, mutual admiration. The mark of true geniuses. Have a good day, Alan. And please don't say 'sort of,' because it's sort of lousy English usage. See you in homeroom, bright and early."

Alan struggled with the double load of books as he walked home, but his mind seemed to move along the treetops. What words! "You're great." "I think you're great." "So much insight for your age." And best of all, "You are strong."

But am I, he wondered. Well if I'm not, I will be. *Sort of!*

121

20

Alan studied Naomi, her eyes, her mouth, her hair. Somewhere, somewhere, he had seen her before. . . . She was squatting on her bed, working on a math problem, wrinkling her nose as she concentrated.

Her books and papers covered the bed and overflowed onto the floor. It reminded Alan of his own room when he studied. And his mother's voice, "A pigpen! Your room is a pigpen! I can't look at it!"

But in all the mix-up of books and papers, Naomi had moved straight ahead. In just two weeks, she'd almost caught up to the class in mathematics and history. Alan was amazed, day after day. How did she *do* it? Maybe she read half the night. Or slept with the books under her pillow. Maybe she was secretly an adult. A genius dwarf.

"Uhkay," she would say when Alan explained something. And even when he'd explained it badly, even when she didn't really seem to be listening, she remembered it.

"Ah, this is very tough problem, number twenty-three," said Naomi, looking up from her work. "Is this stupid

122

river flowing three miles an hour, and this stupid boat goes ten miles an hour in first hour, then goes five miles an hour in second hour, upstream direction . . . Do you have answer?"

Alan searched among his homework papers. "OK, here it is. What answer did *you* get?"

"Four hours and a half."

"That's right! Only three people got it right in the whole class!"

"Is now four," said Naomi, looking at the next problem. She didn't even care! She didn't care that twenty-eight others had gotten it wrong, including Alan himself. It was almost annoying.

"I got the wrong answer, you know," he said.

"Oh. Uhkay, I teach you."

"I know how to do it *now*, Naomi, kid."

"Uhkay, Alan, kid."

They studied in silence for a few minutes. Then an air-raid drill began, the sirens wailing like giants wounded in battle. Naomi gave a tiny scream and jumped under her bed calling, *"Maman! Maman!"*

"It's only practice," called Alan. "Hey, come on out, Naomi!" Was it happening again? A minute ago, everything was completely normal. What should he do? Make it a joke. Make it fun. Somehow.

The lights went out everywhere. Car headlights, window lights, the street lights of New York disappeared into the dark like falling stars.

"Naomi, I've got to turn out the light. The air-raid wardens could arrest the Liebmans if I don't. It's just for a little while, OK?" Alan switched off the light.

Mr. and Mrs. Liebman came into the room with Naomi's mother.

"Where is she?" asked Mr. Liebman.

"Under the bed."

"Naomeleh, it's only nothing," said Mrs. Liebman. "A practice blackout. You don't have to be afraid."

Then Naomi's mother spoke gently to her in French. But Naomi said, *"Non. Non.* I won't!"

"OK," said Alan. "I'll tell you what's going on, since you can't see. This is the news! Yes, ladies and gentlemen, all the light bulbs in New York have been eaten up. The bulb monster has struck again. Would you say a few words into the microphone, Mr. Monster?" Alan changed his voice, making it deeper. "Ah yezzz. I love light bulbzz. Yummm yummm yummm. I love those crunchy, crispy hundred-watt glass potatoes with ketchup."

There was a tiny giggle from under the bed.

"Yezz! And now for some headlights with salt, pepper, and mustard! I must have mustard, 'cause mustard is a must!"

There was another giggle. Mr. Liebman said softly to the others, "Come. Let him be. He's doing better than us."

"And I love to eat streetlights. They're like lollipops on the end of a stick. Lemon lollipops, my favorite flavor. And red traffic lights, cherry flavor. And green traffic lights, lime flavor . . ."

The all-clear sirens sounded and the lights started coming on.

"Oh, I ate too much. Uurgh! My stomach! My

stomaaach! I think I'm going to throw up! Help! Here come the lights! Aaagh! Eeergh! Ooorgh! I'm vomiting all the lights out. Yaaich! Yeerch! There go all the lollipops!"

Alan turned the bedroom light on. From under the bed, Naomi called, "Alan."

"Yes?"

"You are screwball. Is right word, 'screwball'? You told me once, what is screwball."

"That's me, all right."

Look at her, thought Alan. She's perfectly OK. *They* didn't know what to do, and I did!

"Hey, Naomi, kid. Come on out. You can't study under the bed."

"Uhkay." She slid out, then stood up and brushed herself off. "I was much afraid. I am coward."

"No."

"Oui!"

"A little, maybe. Everybody is."

"A lot, *certainement*, I am."

"Well, don't worry. You're safe with me, you know."

"Ah oui. You are smart and brave. And nice. And funny. Is many things for one person. . . . What is word? You are super-duper!"

"No, I'm not."

"Yes, yes, yes. Super-duper."

"Come on. Cut it out."

"Cut it out? From where I cut?"

"That means quit it. Stop."

"Ah. English is crazy language. And crazy people also,

English people. I read in book." She pointed to the open history book on a chair.

"Why are they crazy?"

"Is in chapter on Massashoo . . . I can't say . . ."

"Massachusetts?"

"*Oui*. In Massa-shusetts Bay Colony are crazy Puritans from England, yes? They came to America for freedom, and then they make everybody have to be Puritans, too. I don't like. They would throw me out."

"Maybe not."

"Oh *oui*, yes! They would! I am *bien étrange*— How you say? Peculiar. They wouldn't want me at all."

She was right! She was right! And they would have kicked *him* out, too. Because he was peculiar also. Like her. They would have had to wander in the forest or something, and live on wild berries. Alone, together. Just the two. Screwballs, together.

"Hey, Naomi. You've got something there. What's so great about the Puritans, just 'cause they're in a history book, right?"

"*Oui*. They are *intolérant!*"

Why hadn't he seen that? It was so clear! What a Naomi! And *he* was super-duper? What about her! She saw right through all the baloney, just like his father did. And without the long speeches.

Wow!

21

The last days of October meant that stickball would soon be completely abandoned; it was football weather. And Alan hated football. That Saturday afternoon, some of the boys had left the game to practice dropkicks farther up the block. The football often landed in the stickball-game outfield.

"Hey! Keep that damn football away! That's our territory, McDonnell," shouted Joe Condello.

"Go jump in the lake, Condello," the boy named McDonnell called back.

Condello lunged toward him, but McDonnell retreated.

"That football comes into our territory again, I'll throw it under a trolley car, I swear."

Alan watched Joe spit toward McDonnell as if he were spitting a plug of tobacco. Then Joe turned back to pitch. Alan paced nervously, waiting. He was next at bat. He desperately wanted a hit, at least a double, to end the season right. By the following weekend, when he could play again, it might be too cold. There would be only football then.

Joe Condello, still angry, threw a wild pitch toward the batter at the plate. Shaun Kelly called to Joe, "Hey, give him something good, Condello!" Then he shouted to the batter, "Hey Ralph, baby! Put it over the fence! Home run, Ralphy, baby!"

The batter let several of Condello's wild pitches go by, then swung with all his might. It was a high pop-up, easily caught by Condello.

"One away!" called Condello. "And the great Silverman is up. The powerhouse!"

Alan took his stance at the plate, grinding his shoes down into the pavement as if it were the dirt of a ball field, and took several practice cuts with the bat. At that moment, Naomi and her mother came around the corner, walking toward the Oak Terrace Arms entrance.

"Hey, there goes Frenchie, the nut," the catcher said, just above a whisper, to Alan.

The pitch went by; Alan didn't even look at it. He turned angrily toward Larry Frankel, the catcher.

"What did you say?"

"Huh? I didn't say anything. That was a strike."

Were they all calling her names now? Larry didn't even realize he'd said it. Larry Frankel was usually OK, maybe because he was small. He wasn't a real rat, like some of them, though he used his smallness to get away with things.

Alan saw Naomi looking right at him. *Don't come near!* The moment Alan thought the thought, he hated himself for it. Why shouldn't she come near? She was as good as they were. Better!

From the street Naomi gave a secret wave, her hand half raised, opening and closing her fist twice. Alan waved back the same way.

She understood. She understood not to come near. Maybe it was the secret friends thing. She was great.

Why was he happy about it? He was a coward, that was it. Waving in secret. Hiding her. He wanted to shout: *Hey, Naomi, kid! Come on and watch the game!* He took a breath, but the words wouldn't come. Coward!

Alan swung at the next pitch, putting all his anger into the power of the bat, and with a great *splat* the ball flew over the far trees along the curb.

"Foul!" called Condello.

"Straighten the next one out, Al, baby!" Shaun shouted.

It may have been a foul, but it was the hardest shot he'd ever hit. Alan felt a little better. Frenchie, the nut, hey? Frankel, the louse!

"Hey, Frankel," Alan whispered to the catcher. "How'd you like me to call you Smelly Frankelly?"

"Better not, Silverman," Larry whispered back.

"Then don't call her Frenchie, the nut."

"OK. So what do you want to call her?"

"Naomi. You got it?"

"Got it."

"Hey, break it up!" shouted Condello. "Let's play ball!"

Alan was amazed. Had Larry agreed because Alan was a little taller? Was Larry afraid of him? Could somebody actually be afraid of him?

The next pitch came in right over the plate, while Alan

was still thinking.

"Strike!" called Larry Frankel.

"You're out, Powerhouse Silverman!" Joe Condello shouted.

Alan dropped the bat and walked back to the curb without any of his usual mutterings. It was the happiest strikeout of his life, last game of the season or not. And if any of the others said something about Naomi, he'd take care of *them*, too.

The next batter hit a high fly ball to the outfield and the game was over. Most of the boys, including Shaun, strolled over to the football group, but Alan picked up his bat and walked to the Oak Terrace Arms lobby. Football was hopeless for him. Maybe Shaun would show him how to toss a football better. Maybe tomorrow.

"Why are you so flushed?" Alan's mother asked him the moment he entered the apartment.

It was a familiar question. It seemed to Alan that when his mother ran out of her usual questions—"Why don't you eat?" "Why are you up so late?" "Why are you biting your lip so much?"—she resorted to "Why are you flushed?"

"I'm flushed," said Alan, "because I just beat up Finch, the janitor, and made him drink his bottle of ammonia."

"Fresh! Fresh answers, I don't need."

"Well I did! It'll be in the papers tomorrow. Wait and see. When the police come, then you'll believe me."

"All right, Alan! Enough! Listen. We have to ask you another thing to do."

"Now what!"

"You won't like it. But still, it has to be done. *Oy, Gott*, I wish your father was home. He has a way of explaining."

"Just *tell* me, Mom, please! Even if I have to jump off the top of the Empire State Building."

"Maybe it's worse, knowing you. . . . All right. Listen. You have to go out, somehow, and play, or take a walk, or do something outside the house with Naomi."

It was incredible! Could his mother read his mind? He'd just been thinking about that secret hand wave again.

"I got it from Mrs. Liebman yesterday. Naomi's afraid to go in the street without her mother. She has to be able to go out. Alan, please. The doctor says so. You could do it very early tomorrow morning. All the boys sleep late, or else they're in church. There's no one in the street early Sunday. Nobody will see you."

Alan sat down at the kitchen table. "OK, you don't have to make a big deal out of it. I'll do it, OK?" And if the guys don't like it, they can lump it, thought Alan. Including Shaun.

His mother looked at him with astonishment. "What? OK? You said OK?"

"No, I said *nokay*. That means 'no, I will.' It's a real word in the dictionary."

"You're making me crazy, Alan! That also is a real word in the dictionary. But you said yes, yes?"

"Yes."

"A miracle. Without a fight? *Oy, Gott.* My heart can't take it. Alan, are you sure you're all right? You *are* flushed."

"I know," said Alan. "Mr. Finch put up a terrific fight."

"Meshuggener."

"You bet."

Alan went to his room and sat down at his desk to check the Piper Cub. Some glued wing struts were drying after a major repair. Maybe he and Shaun could fly planes tomorrow afternoon and the heck with learning to throw a football. It was funny how things happened, Alan thought. Just a few weeks ago, he would have screamed and ranted at the very idea of marching along the street with Naomi. But now . . . he almost wanted to. He could show her things, and sort of be her protector and advisor. She probably didn't know anything about the neighborhood, except maybe where the grocery was.

Alan touched up a loose strut with more glue. . . . Then he suddenly realized. The plane! Of course! He could walk with Naomi to Holmes Airport! *They* could fly the plane! They could really have fun!

Alan rushed back to the kitchen and told his mother his idea.

"Alan, it's too far," she said. "It takes hours."

"That's walking the way *you* walk, not the way *I* walk."

"Listen, it's a good idea maybe for some other time, but—"

"Why can't you at least ask her mother? Or Mrs. Lieb-

132

man. Or Mr. Liebman. Or whoever is the boss there. You're always having secret conferences. Have a conference!"

"All right. I'll ask. No harm in asking. I'll ask. Why not? . . . I'll be right back."

Alan paced back and forth in the kitchen while his mother was upstairs. He took a quick look in the refrigerator, but there was nothing worth raiding except the sliced corned beef. And the corned beef was for supper. . . . Alan took a huge slice and crammed it into his mouth. He was still chewing when his mother returned.

"What's that you're eating, Alan?"

"What'd they say?"

"Is that the corned beef, Alan?"

"What'd they *say*?"

"They said all right, but you should call them on the phone when you get there. To make sure everything is OK."

"But there's no phones there. It's just a big field."

"So go to the nearest candy store or drugstore." His mother opened the refrigerator door and looked inside. "Alan, that *is* the corned beef!"

Alan swallowed the last of the huge slice he had taken. "No. It *was* the corned beef."

"Wisenheimer!"

Alan dodged his mother's swat at him and raced to his room to check out the Piper Cub again. It was ready to fly. He raised the plane over his desk, slowly, slowly, and flew it around the room, into the clouds. *ALAN SIL-*

133

VERMAN, NOTED AVIATOR, COMPLETED THE FINAL LEG OF HIS RECORD-BREAKING ROUND-THE-WORLD FLIGHT WITH HIS FIANCEE, NAOMI, BESIDE HIM. "IT WAS NOTHING" WERE HIS WORDS ON CRASH-LANDING SAFELY AT HOLMES AIRPORT. DETAILS AND PHOTOS ON PAGE SEVENTEEN.

22

"Aren't you ready yet?" Alan's mother called toward his room. "She'll be here any minute!"

"I'm ready! I'm ready!" Alan called back. Why was she always so nervous whenever people were coming or going anywhere? What if he were a minute late? Couldn't they wait one minute!

"Alan! Hurry already!" His mother appeared at his bedroom door, her hair wild and uncombed. She looks like a witch, thought Alan. She'll scare Naomi to death.

"For crying out loud!" he shouted. "I've got to get my repair kit together! What in hell do you want from me?"

"Watch your mouth! That freshness! And that language!"

"You think that's something! Come and watch a stickball game someday. You may learn a couple of words that you never knew were invented even."

"I hear plenty through the window! Plenty! Everybody in the house hears! It's disgusting. And there's girls playing there, too!"

"Well, it's not me!"

"I know."

"That's 'cause I'm *lovely*!"

"Enough already! I don't need from you this kind of aggravation! Your father is sleeping; let him sleep! He works hard enough all week! What *is* with you! You don't want to go with her for this walk; so say it! Don't give me all this—this—this *kvetching*! This *tummel*!"

"I *do* want to go! What do you think of that? I just don't want to be rushed—"

The doorbell rang. Alan's mother pushed her hair back, and pointed to Alan to go to the door.

"My hair isn't even combed. Alan, please."

"My hair isn't combed either."

"Alan!"

Alan opened the door, still angry. Naomi was holding her mother's hand. Like a two-year-old, thought Alan. She was wearing her green sweater with the buttons down the front. In her hand was a brown paper bag. I *hate* green sweaters, thought Alan. It's a horrible sweater! Nobody wears sweaters like that! And what's in that paper bag? Not her doll! Anything but that!

"I'll be right back," said Alan abruptly. He rushed to get his plane and repair kit, then said, "OK, let's go!" He knew he sounded grouchy, because that was exactly how he felt.

"Uhkay," said Naomi. Mrs. Kirshenbaum gave Naomi's sweater a straightening tug, then kissed her.

Alan followed Naomi down the stairs. Why couldn't she go faster? What if Shaun opened his door? Or anyone!

He didn't care, of course. But still!

They reached the lobby, and Naomi stopped at the big glass door. What was wrong with her? Did she expect him to open the door for her? Open it yourself.

But she didn't move. Alan put down his model plane and opened the door, but Naomi just stood there. She looked frightened, as if the street were a river into which she had to plunge from a great height.

"Come on, Naomi, kid. *I'm* here. It's only a stupid sidewalk."

Naomi walked a few steps out to the street, then halted, looking back toward Alan. She was like a little child waiting for its parent.

Alan felt ashamed. She needed him, and he was acting like a rat. He said, as pleasantly as he could, "OK, Naomi, kid. We're on our way to my favorite place. Holmes Airport. Only it's not an airport anymore. But it's still my favorite."

As they walked, he noticed that she paced herself to be just a half step behind him. When he paused at the curb before crossing, she paused. When he rushed across, she rushed. Like a little child.

Once they were a few blocks from the Oak Terrace Arms, Alan started walking more slowly. None of the boys on his block were likely to see them now. Naomi adjusted her pace again, to be just a little behind him.

Then Alan saw the hobby store where he bought most of his models. Even on Sunday, a small-scale train went round and round in the window, disappearing under a mountain and reappearing at a village.

"Look at that," called Alan.

"Oh! *C'est joli!* It is a whole little village," Naomi said, pressing against the window.

"Someday I'm going to get a set like that," Alan said. "But it costs a lot."

"I knew once a boy had a train just like—" Naomi stopped. "I never knew a boy. . . . No, I never knew . . ." She walked away from the window, then turned back toward Alan, as if pleading for him to follow.

"What's wrong?" Alan asked as he joined her. "You look sort of scared. . . ."

"Is nothing. Don't ask me please any questions. Please!" She started to walk.

Alan wondered if it had anything to do with Europe. In all the time they'd been together, she'd never talked about Europe.

They continued walking. Naomi seemed lost in thought, so Alan just whistled softly to himself. And in a little while, Naomi started whistling, too.

It took well over an hour to reach Holmes Airport, and another ten minutes before Alan found a phone booth in a drugstore. He called the Liebmans and told Mrs. Liebman that everything was fine; Naomi didn't seem frightened at all. He didn't mention how the sight of that model train had disturbed her. Why trouble them; she seemed perfectly all right now.

Then Alan ran with Naomi out onto the great open field.

"Alan! Is *magnifique*! So big a space. The sky is all over!"

"I'll race you!" Alan shouted. "Come on, Naomi! We have to get to the middle of the field."

"I'm coming! Wait! You are too fast!"

"This is it!" Alan shouted as he finally stopped. "Holmes Airport!"

Naomi turned and gazed in every direction, one arm around her paper bag, one hand shielding her eyes from the morning sun. The wind from the west rippled through the tall grass.

"Is tremendous. . . . But I do not see airport," said Naomi, confused.

"This! This is it! You're on it! This is Holmes Airport!"

"But is just big, huge, empty field. Where are the airplanes?"

"They're gone. But this used to be the biggest airport in the city," he said. "See there? That long stretch with only patches of low grass? That was the main landing strip. That's where we'll fly the Piper Cub. Come on!"

They walked out to the center of the landing strip, and Alan put his repair kit on the gravel. Naomi set her brown paper bag down next to the kit.

"What's in that?" asked Alan.

"It is surprise," said Naomi.

"Can I look?"

"*Non*. Later. It is something to eat."

"Really? Like what?"

Alan felt his stomach tighten with hunger, but he did

want to get the plane up. The wind was perfect now.

"OK," he said. "Now watch. I'm winding the propeller. See?"

Naomi watched as Alan twirled the propeller with his finger, round and round. He kept count of the turns, ". . . 301, 302, 303, 304 . . ."

When he reached 700, he stopped winding, checked the wind, then raised the plane a little higher than his head, with one hand over the propeller to keep it from spinning.

"OK," he said. "Here goes. Takeoff!"

The plane flew up in a wide turn, and headed toward the sun. Naomi ran along the landing strip, trying to follow. She called upward, "Hey, yellow bird! Wait for me! Hey, *oiseau jaune!*"

Alan watched as the Piper Cub continued its slow turn and headed north.

"I am faster than the plane, Alan! Look! Alan!"

She ran along the field, calling, leaping, almost dancing, while the plane circled above her.

For a second, Alan pictured her on her bed, tearing those pieces of paper. And then with Yvette, the doll. His father was right. She hadn't been alive. He wished his father could see her now. And Mrs. Liebman and Mrs. Kirshenbaum. Everyone.

"You are making me dizzy, crazy airplane! Hey, come back!" called Naomi.

As the plane started coming down, she waved her arms wildly and shouted. "Hey, *oiseau jaune! Je suis ici!* I'm over here!"

140

The plane landed among weeds, and Naomi raced to it, reaching it well before Alan. But she hesitated to touch it. Alan came up beside her and knelt by the plane.

"Is it broken?" asked Naomi, anxiously.

"Let me see. . . . No. A little tear in the wing, that's all. I can fix that easy. Come on, I need my repair kit."

Within a few minutes, Alan had glued a thin strip of tissue paper over the tear, and the plane was ready again.

"OK, Naomi, kid. This time you do it."

"Me?"

"Sure. Here, hold the plane."

Alan showed her how to wind the propeller with a quick, even movement of one finger. Then he showed her how to stand and launch the plane.

"Go ahead. Let her go!"

"Now?"

"Now!"

"*Bon voyage!*" She released the plane, and it climbed rapidly in another great loop around the field. And again, Naomi ran after the plane, jumping when it seemed to be descending too fast, then shouting as it lifted again on another wave of air.

This time, the plane made a perfect landing only ten feet away from Naomi. She watched the wheels kick up tiny clouds of dust from the ground, just like a real plane.

"Oh see! *C'est épatant!* Alan, look how good!"

They flew the plane again and again, until Naomi's voice was hoarse from shouting, and Alan was exhausted from running with her. Where did she get such energy?

They sat down and admired the plane, which had come through all the flights with almost no damage.

"You should give it a name," said Naomi.

"Like what?" asked Alan.

"*Oiseau jaune.*"

"What does *that* mean?"

"Yellow bird. Call it *L'Oiseau jaune.*"

"OK. That's the name of the plane. *L'Oiseau jaune.* Shaun will think— Well, I won't tell him."

"Who is Shaun?"

"Uh . . . He's just a friend of mine."

"He lives on second floor?"

"That's right! How did you know?"

"I see him with you. He also has airplane, yes? You remember, in the lobby? He called me Crazy Cat. He said, 'Here comes Crazy Cat.'"

Alan was speechless. She had heard it! The lobby was a tricky place to whisper; the whispers echoed all over. What could he say!

"I don't care," said Naomi. "Alan, I don't care. I don't."

"He, you know, he says things. . . . Like he makes up names, even for me, but he doesn't mean anything."

"There is a comic strip, Crazy Cat, *oui*?"

"I guess so."

"I don't care. I am crazy, you know."

Was she? No! But how could she *say* that? As if it were nothing much. Like having a sore throat. . . . She *wasn't* crazy. It was impossible. Crazy people didn't know they were crazy. Everyone knew *that*. She was too smart, too funny, too everything, to be crazy.

"You're OK. There's nothing wrong with you. . . . Hey, let's see what's in your paper bag."

"Uhkay. Close your eyes."

Alan heard the bag being torn open. Naomi seemed to be fixing something.

"Uhkay. Look."

Spread out before him on a big red napkin was a miniature feast. There were a dozen tiny triple-decker sandwiches, and a paper cup full of tomato chunks and olives. Around these were little cakes with icing: lemon, strawberry, chocolate. And at the side were a small bottle of milk and more paper cups.

"It's beautiful!" said Alan. "Boy, your mother sure knows how to make a picnic lunch."

"Not *ma mère*. I make it."

"You're kidding."

"Is easy. I show you someday."

"I hate to eat it," said Alan. "It looks so great! But . . . let's eat it anyway."

The food tasted just as good as it looked, and Alan wondered if Naomi's being French was why it was so elegant and different. When his mother made a sandwich it was loaded, but it never had the cool, delicate softness that these sandwiches had.

"This is really great," said Alan, taking his third cake. "But you shouldn't have spent all the time on it. You didn't have to get so fancy and all."

"Why not? You are my friend."

"Still—"

"*Non*, it was nothing. I used to make picnics with my friends. Was long time ago. We played picnic in the courtyard. We had toy dishes and cups. . . . My friends . . . they are all dead now, *oui*?"

"No!" said Alan. "I mean, maybe not. . . ."

Alan thought of all the newsreels and photos: burning houses in London, Nazi troops marching, people pushed into trucks. The fall of France, of Paris. Naomi had been there. What had she *seen*?

He wanted to ask. He wanted to know. But be careful, he thought. Let her talk if she wants to talk. But be careful!

23

Naomi clasped her knees and stared at the ground, deep in thought. The breeze blew some hair free, over her cheek. With her dark eyes, and her thin, dark face, Alan thought she looked beautiful. Where had he seen that face before? He could never remember.

"Yes, they are dead," said Naomi, after a long pause. "I think so. . . ."

"Maybe you'll see them again, you know, after the war is over," Alan said quickly.

"The war *is* over," said Naomi.

"No . . . I mean, it won't be too long now. The Allies are across the German border."

"*Ah oui.*" She said it without any expression.

"Should we talk about something else?" asked Alan.

"I killed my father, you know." The words came at him and coiled round him like a poisonous snake. Alan was afraid to speak; whatever he said would be wrong.

"I . . . I . . ." He couldn't think. He knew he was

stuttering. She *was* crazy! "I thought he was k-killed by the Nazis."

"*Ah oui.*"

"*Wasn't* he?"

"But I helped them. . . ."

"N-Naomi, that's not true!"

"I am liar? How do you know? Tell me! You were there? You were *there*?"

"No . . . No . . ."

"All the maps. I killed him with the maps. You see? All the maps! The maps!" Her eyes were wide; her fists opened and closed as she spoke.

Don't be scared, thought Alan. You jerk, don't get scared now! Easy. Take it easy. But she looks . . . she looks insane! She does!

"Naomi, k-kid. I-I don't understand. About maps and all. But you don't have to tell me. Just, please, Naomi, please. . . . Everything's OK now. Just sort of take it easy. . . . Please . . ."

Naomi looked straight ahead, past Alan, toward something in her mind.

"My father! He said we have to tear up all the maps! Of the sewers! They went through the sewers. The Resistance soldiers. My father made the maps. Of the Paris sewers. He said we have to tear up all the maps. I . . . I . . . At night. The Resistance soldiers. They attack the Gestapo at night. And they escape through the sewers. But the Nazis find out. My father is making maps. They find out. And they come! They come! Look! Two trucks in the street! My father says, 'Tear up the maps! Naomi,

146

tear up the maps! And flush them down the toilet. Tear up all the maps!' We tear! We tear! Our fingernails break! Our hands are covered with blood! I tear, I chew, I eat the maps! No more! I CAN'T! NO MORE! But the Nazis are at the door! *Vite! Vite!* Tear! Tear! Tear! Faster! Faster! Then he pushes me under the bed. And they hammer! And they break in the door! . . . *Look!* They beat him with clubs! They beat him on the floor! His head is covered with blood! Everywhere is blood! Is blood under the bed! All over! All over! Blood! . . . I tore! I tore the maps! I didn't tear enough! I didn't! I couldn't! . . . They leave. They're gone. The Nazis are gone. Listen! . . . So quiet. Shh! So very quiet. Maybe is all right. Maybe he is just sleeping, my father. . . . Then he says, very weak, 'Naomi.' He says, 'Naomi. Naomi. Naomi.' And he falls asleep. I try to wake him up. He is dead! HE IS DEAD! *HE IS DEAD!* I TORE! I TORE! I TORE! NOT ENOUGH! NOT ENOUGH!—"

"Naomi, stop! You couldn't help it! Stop! It's the Nazis! The Nazis! Naomi! *You couldn't help it!*"

"See, look. My hands are clean. My dress is clean. He is dead, that's all. So much blood . . ."

"Oh Naomi. Naomi . . ."

Alan put his hand on her shoulder, then on her head, gently, the way his rabbi did when giving a blessing. The words moved through his mind, the old words. May the Lord bless you and keep you. May the Lord let his countenance shine upon you, and give you peace. For her, he thought. For her.

"You're . . . you're safe now, Naomi. OK? You're

safe. No one . . . no one is going to hurt you anymore.
I won't let anybody hurt you. OK, Naomi? . . . OK?"

"Uhkay."

"When you want, just come over to me in the street, or anywhere. If anyone bothers you, or you just want to talk, or anything. OK?"

"Uhkay."

"Don't be afraid anymore. OK, Naomi?"

"Uhkay."

24

They walked back slowly. Naomi didn't speak, but she glanced at Alan from time to time, as if to make sure he was still there beside her.

Again Alan had the eerie feeling that he'd seen or known a girl like her before. With large dark eyes like hers. The edge of a thought flickered. It had had something to do with the Nazis. Something to do with a roundup of Jews by the Nazis. Wait a minute . . . wait. . . .

Then, at last, Alan remembered. He had been watching a newsreel at the movies; the one that had made his father weep. There had been a girl with large dark eyes, a girl being forced into a truck by Nazi soldiers. She had raised her head and looked right at the camera for a split second. Her face had been Naomi's face: her forehead, her eyes, her sadness. There had been dozens of Jews being forced into the truck, to be sent to a concentration camp. But that girl had looked straight at Alan, and Alan had twisted in his seat, wanting desperately to help her.

It couldn't have been Naomi; it had happened in Warsaw, Poland. Yet it *was* Naomi. The newsreel seemed to Alan to be happening here, to be happening now, in Queens, New York.

That truck parked down the block could just as well be a Nazi truck, he thought. That gray building could be Gestapo headquarters. We could be walking home in Warsaw right now. We could. It would be Sunday. Everything nice and peaceful. She's wearing that green sweater, just like now. The sun is shining, just like now. And that truck moves slowly up the block and stops in front of us. And we get pushed into the truck. And no one knows. And no one cares.

Who cares about anything, anyway? Crazy Cat, Frenchie-the-nut, that's what they call her. Her father stood up to the Nazis. He was a hero. And so was she! So was she! Tearing maps until her hands were covered with blood.

Alan suddenly remembered the map of New York in the hallway. The map with the red lines. All the scraps of paper. All the tearing. She was trying to save his life! All that time, she was still trying to save his life!

Naomi hesitated at a street corner. A police car had passed down the next block, its siren screaming. She looked at Alan, frightened.

"It's OK," said Alan. "Just the cops chasing themselves around the block."

Alan took her hand and held it as they crossed the street. Her hand felt small in his. It made Alan feel good, like an adult, a heroic adult. He held her hand for the next entire block. Then, balancing his plane and repair kit in his free arm, he began to swing her hand back and forth, higher and higher. Naomi couldn't help smiling.

Quick as a shutter clicking in a camera, Alan thought of the dark-eyed girl in the newsreel. He was holding *her* hand. And for a fraction of a second, the dark-eyed girl smiled, too. Then the shutter closed, and she was gone.

Alan swung Naomi's hand up over their heads and around in a circle, and another, like a Ferris wheel, releasing and holding, up and around, again and again, and Naomi was laughing and crying out, "*Arrête!* You are crazy! Alan! Help!" and she was better, she was laughing, she was herself, she was Naomi. They were here, in New York City, in Queens.

And the Nazis were gone.

Alan started "flying" the plane in front of Naomi. He put the plane through barrel rolls and loop-the-loops, then flew it backward. Naomi tried to catch the plane, but Alan flew it out of reach.

"Can I fly it?" she called.

Keep it up, thought Alan. Keep it going. "Got to catch it first," said Alan, teasing her. "Can't catch a yellow bird."

"Oh, *oui*, I can."

"OK, let's see you."

Naomi raced after Alan as he ran with the plane over his head. Then he suddenly stopped short and made the plane swoop down and land on top of her head.

"Ran out of fuel," said Alan. "Crash landing. Sorry."

Naomi started "flying" the plane, making it dip and rise above the pavement. But as they neared the store with the train in the window, Alan noticed that she purposely flew the plane out to the curb. She was clearly trying to avoid that window. She held the plane up high and flew it along the edge of the sidewalk, over the parked cars. When they stopped for traffic at the next corner, Naomi continued to fly the plane in little circles above her head.

It was then that Alan saw Shaun, a block behind them. He must have been following at a distance. Alan blinked and stared at him, while Naomi, unmindful, kept flying the plane. Shaun walked toward them, then hesitated and stopped.

"OK, Silverman!" Shaun called.

"What?" Alan called back.

"You'll see what!"

Naomi turned. "What is matter?" she asked Alan.

"I don't know," Alan answered. "Come on! Let's go." He took her by her arm and led her across the street as fast as he could.

"Sissy!" called Shaun, from a distance.

Alan kept walking with Naomi, his fist clenched. Why did Shaun have to sneak around like that? He was a sneak! Crazy Cat! Frenchie! Sissy! The hell with them all! He could walk with anyone he wanted to walk with. Anyone!

"Alan, please? You are angry at him?" asked Naomi.

"Yes!"

"What did he do?"

"He called me a sissy."

"What is sissy? Is it like coward?"

"I can't explain."

"You are angry, also, at me?"

"No! Of course not!" Alan took a breath, and forced himself to speak calmly. "I'm not angry at you, Naomi. I just have problems like everybody else. Don't worry about it, OK?"

"I am sorry. . . ."

They had reached the Oak Terrace Arms. Alan pushed the door open and walked with Naomi through the lobby in glum silence. Why was he so angry at Shaun? Because of the sissy business? No! He *wasn't* a sissy. Shaun could call him that till he was blue in the face. It didn't matter anymore. It was just that Shaun was so great sometimes. So great. And so damned stupid other times. Like now!

25

On Monday morning, Alan waited for Shaun in front of the house, hoping to be able to talk to him, to explain, on the way to school. But Shaun must have left early. Purposely, because Shaun never left early.

Alan started walking to school alone. His breath turned white in the first chill of autumn. On a better morning, he would have hissed to create the steam of a locomotive, or would have blown a long plume for the smoking edge of a downed Messerschmitt. He remembered how, last fall, he and Shaun had "smoked" imaginary cigarettes in little puffs.

Alan started whistling. He whistled to show anyone who saw him that all was well, that he liked walking to school alone, that it was great weather, and it was a great day, and if Shaun didn't want to walk to school with him, he could go to hell!

Then Alan saw Shaun up ahead, walking with Tony Ferrara. What were they laughing at? Was Shaun talking about him? *Alan Silverman flies model planes with girls, you know. Alan Silverman's a sissy. Alan Silverman plays with Crazy Cat.* Didn't Tony just turn back to glance at him? What were they *saying*?

Alan pressed his books against his side and started walking as fast as he could. Shaun wasn't going to get away with this! If he has something to say, thought Alan, let him say it to *me*!

Alan drew alongside of Tony. "Hi," said Alan, glumly.

"How's it going," Tony mumbled.

Shaun stared at Alan angrily, but said nothing.

"Test in history," said Alan to the air in front of him.

"Yeah," said Tony. "Don't remind me."

"All you have to know," Alan continued, "is that the Pilgrims landed at the foot of Manhattan Island and called the colony Jamestown in honor of Queen Mary—"

"What the hell do you want!" Shaun bellowed. "What do you want, Silverman!"

"Nothing."

"Then leave me alone!"

"I just want to talk a minute."

"Talk? I ought to beat your brains out!"

Shaun started striding angrily in another direction. Alan turned and followed him, while Tony, bewildered, shrugged and kept walking toward school.

"Quit following me, Silverman! Scram!"

"Shaun, for crying out loud! Listen for a minute! Give me a *minute*!"

Shaun stopped walking, took off his wristwatch, studied it a moment, then said, "OK. You've got one minute!"

"All right," Alan said. "I'm gonna talk fast, OK? I've

155

been sort of helping her for the last couple of months. I couldn't tell you. But I had to do it. She's got something, you know, wrong with her. Because of the war. Because of Hitler. The Nazis killed her father. Right in front of her eyes. He was all covered with blood and everything. He was in the French Resistance. And they killed him. It drove her out of her mind, sort of. And they needed someone to help her. I had to help. I'm *glad* I helped. Shaun, she's great. You'd like her. She's really great. She's funny, and smart, and everything. My errand. That was my errand. . . . You're not even listening. OK, I owe you two dollars. I lost that bet. . . . I guess that's my minute."

"You've got eighteen seconds more," Shaun said coldly, staring at his watch.

"Shaun you know me pretty good. I'm telling you the truth. I liked playing stickball a lot. I didn't want to quit playing stickball. It was almost like, you know, a matter of life and death. It was—"

"The minute's up! OK, Silverman, now *I* get a minute! And you'd better listen, you son of a bitch!"

"Shaun, I—"

"Listen, Silverman! You just said you're telling the truth. But you're a liar—"

"I'm not lying—"

"Shut up! I gave you a minute! Now you give *me* a minute! . . . Out at the airport, remember? *Maybe* she can speak good English, you said. Her name is Naomi, you *heard*. And your errand. It's a family thing. You're a liar! You could have told me all this stuff back then. But you lied."

156

"But you kept calling me a sissy!"

"I never called you that."

"You would have! You kept saying things about playing with girls. And you *did* call me a sissy. Yesterday. Out on the street, in front of everybody."

"There was nobody around. And I was sore!"

"And you called her Crazy Cat!"

"I was just kidding. She seemed crazy, that's all. You could have told me what was wrong with her. But no. You lied instead!"

"I didn't lie! I just . . . I don't know."

"You just didn't trust me. I'm your stickball friend. Right? Your model-airplane friend. But I'm not your *friend!*"

In a flash of pain, Alan saw that Shaun was right. He *hadn't* trusted him. He had lied. He hadn't trusted that Shaun would understand; that Shaun wasn't Joe Condello.

Alan fought to keep from crying. He must not cry! . . . Or was he still not trusting Shaun?

"Shaun . . . I—" Alan swallowed hard. "I was wrong. Dead wrong. . . . I'm . . . I'm sorry. . . ."

"Well, I'm *not!* I'm glad I found out. Like I said, I do what I want. . . . Look, I'm not gonna bother you, Silverman. I'm not going to get in your way, OK? But just stay the hell out of *my* way. You want to play stickball? Great. Go on the other team. I won't bother you. You want to fly planes? Fly them with *her.* And you don't have to worry; I never called her Crazy Cat to no one. I said that to you, *only* to you, because I thought that it was like . . . I could say anything to you. . . ."

Alan saw that Shaun was trying not to cry, himself.

"I could say anything to you, because we were like—like brothers almost. Well I was *wrong*! So just stay out of my way, and I'll stay out of yours. OK? That's a deal! . . . You got me late for school, but I don't care. Let her mark me late. There's more important things than being late for school. But you—! You'll probably go and kiss Mrs. Landley's behind! So long, Silverman!"

Shaun wheeled around, and stalked off toward school. Alan stood without moving, wishing there were some magic thing he could do that would change everything.

As the mist of his breath became tears in his eyes, the world blurred. Shaun would never have called him a sissy for helping Naomi. And he would never have called her names. Had Shaun been in his place, he would have helped Naomi, too.

How could he have been so *stupid!*?

26

Alan and Shaun avoided each other in school and in the street. To make matters worse, Joe Condello had sensed something was wrong between them, and had started taunting Alan on the way to school.

"Hey, Silverman! Where's the soapsuds twin? Where's your bodyguard? Hey, I'm asking you a question."

Alan would bite his lip, look straight ahead, and ignore him. It seemed to work; Joe Condello lost interest very quickly when Alan didn't answer. But every so often, he started again, testing Alan with a new set of insults. And at the end of each session, he would spit and walk away. It seemed almost funny to Alan that he could tell when the taunting was about to end, by Condello's spitting.

Though school was dreary without Shaun, it was a joy to be with Naomi. She seemed happier than ever. On Tuesday, after they'd finished studying together, she surprised Alan with another picnic, spread out on the Liebmans' dining-room table. This time she had made what she called "a cuckoo picnic."

She'd prepared little frozen sandwiches, with layers of cheese, cucumbers, and ice cream. And there were crackers with four small dabs of mustard, ketchup, mayonnaise, and pickle relish on each. Her strangest concoction, Alan thought, was hard-boiled eggs stuffed with shredded mint chocolate.

On another afternoon, Naomi showed Alan how to stretch a thread across the living room, from the ceiling at one end to the floor at the other. She placed hairpins on the high end of the thread, and they slid down, right across the room. Naomi pretended the hairpins were survivors of a sinking clipper ship, being safely carried to shore on a lifeline, a breeches buoy. Naomi mentioned, without emotion, that she had done this as a little girl in France.

That Friday, with no urgent homework to be done, Alan spent the entire evening with Naomi, having dinner at the Liebmans'. Naomi had made the dessert: lemon pie. Alan tried to show her how great it was by having three helpings.

After dinner, Mr. Liebman suggested that they all go to a movie. There was a Marx Brothers movie, *A Day at the Races*, playing at a nearby theater, and it would do them all good to get out. Alan had seen the picture years ago, but he couldn't wait to see it again.

Naomi rocked in her seat with laughter, and though she scarcely understood English, Mrs. Kirshenbaum laughed, too. The Marx Brothers needed no language to be understood.

Every time Harpo Marx appeared, Naomi grabbed

Alan's arm and started laughing again.

"Alan, help! He is so cuckoo!" she said.

"I can't laugh anymore," said Alan. "I ate too much pie."

"Oh, poor Alan! I laugh for both of us!"

On the way home, they stopped for ice-cream sodas. And to be as crazy as Harpo, Alan started blowing bubbles into his soda through his straw. Naomi immediately did the same. As their glasses filled with froth and overflowed onto the counter, Alan expected one of the adults to tell them to stop. But instead, they seemed delighted that Naomi was misbehaving, as if this were part of her being better.

"I have a vanilla *volcan*," said Naomi.

"*Volcan?*" asked Alan.

"*Oui, c'est un volcan vanille.* What erupts, poofhh! *Volcan.*"

"Oh, you mean 'volcano,' " said Alan.

Then the counterman gave them a very ugly look, and they stopped their volcanoes, but started a pepper war, trying to pour pepper into each other's sodas. When Alan couldn't get past Naomi's defense, he suddenly turned and shook a generous downpour of pepper into Mr. Liebman's soda.

"Alan," said Mr. Liebman, "I have very bad news for you. I happen to like pepper in my soda. It was flat. Very flat. Now it's perfect."

Naomi and Alan laughed, but Alan regretted that he'd done it. He knew that in the eyes of Mr. and Mrs. Liebman he could do no wrong, because of his helping Naomi.

161

He was taking advantage, and he knew it.

"I'm sorry," said Alan, very seriously.

Mr. Liebman said, softly, so Naomi couldn't hear, "Alan, this is good. Some fun, some mischief. You think I can't take a little . . . uh . . . uh . . . a little pep . . . pep . . ." Mr. Liebman sneezed violently.

"That's a lot better than Greenspan's snuff that he passes around at Services," said Mr. Liebman. "Now *that's* what I call a cherry soda." And to their astonishment, he drank the entire soda in one sweep. It had been a great evening.

But on Saturday, Naomi had to go to Manhattan with her mother and Mrs. Liebman for her regular visit to the doctor. Alan felt alone and friendless. His mother was visiting an aunt in the hospital, and his father was at a friend's house, helping with some committee work for the synagogue. The apartment was empty. Alan went from room to room, searching for something to do. It was only twelve-thirty. Naomi wouldn't be back till three or four.

He could work on the Piper Cub. No, he wasn't in the mood. . . . He could finish *The Hound of the Baskervilles*. Why bother? He'd seen the movie, and knew the ending. . . . He could do homework. Too early in the weekend. . . .

Alan heard the shouts from a football game in progress down below. It was no use; he couldn't throw a football. And even if he could, Condello wouldn't take him, and Shaun . . . He didn't want to think about Shaun.

Alan moped. He sat in the armchair studying the ceiling, and saw that the blemishes in the plaster formed a reasonably good picture of a giraffe. Then he opened his history textbook and studied the names of all its previous owners. Jeanne Marcus, Frederic Klausner, Joseph H. Battista, Robert Denton, Maryann Carmiglia. Alan Silverman. Alan added "Esq." after his name; it was a sign of distinction, and his name certainly stood out distinctly now.

He wandered around the house. He took out his hidden collection of pinup pictures cut from newspapers, and took it into the bathroom. Afterward he went to the kitchen and ate two pieces of cold fried chicken. Then he stared at the living-room ceiling again. Not really a giraffe; more like a turtle with a very long neck. Or possibly a monster from Mars.

His mother returned at three with a totally boring account of his aunt's gall-bladder operation. Finally, at three-thirty, Mrs. Liebman appeared at the door, bursting with news. While Alan's mother put up coffee, Mrs. Liebman told them that the doctor had said Naomi could start school that very next Monday.

"She's so happy, you can't imagine. Alan, you'll come upstairs to see her, yes? Such good news! I'm telling you, I'm beside myself! . . . Ruth, your coffee is boiling over."

"She'll be in all my classes, right?" asked Alan.

"Of course!" said Mrs. Liebman. "We've been in twice now to see the principal. Everything is prepared. And you, Alan . . . You can be proud. It was only with your help, believe me. Your name is inscribed in the Book of Life. I'm telling you, God sees everything."

Alan couldn't help thinking of his pinup pictures, and winced slightly.

"Still, Alan," Mrs. Liebman continued, "there's one last thing I have to ask. One last favor to me. To walk with her to school, Alan. To see she's all right. At least, for a while."

Favor to *her*? What about *Naomi*, thought Alan. Doesn't she think I'd do it for Naomi, for crying out loud? Or does she think I'm doing it for her lousy chocolate bars?

As if she could read his thoughts, Alan's mother murmured in a warning voice, "Alan . . ."

Mrs. Liebman said, almost in tears, "I ask you as a favor to me, Alan. . . . Please . . ."

Alan spoke very carefully. "I won't do it as a favor to you, Mrs. Liebman—"

"ALAN!" his mother said, sharply.

Alan continued, "I lost a friend because of this. I wouldn't lose a friend, for *you*. You've got friends. Like my mother is your friend. I see you talking to people all day long. You've got plenty of friends, and I don't! . . . When I do something, it's for Naomi, OK? Not for you. I'm not doing anything for you."

Mrs. Liebman nodded her head in silent assent, three or four times. "I understand . . . I understand. . . . Thank you, Alan—"

"DON'T THANK ME!"

In shocked silence, Mrs. Liebman looked toward Alan's mother.

"I don't know," said his mother. "His father, maybe,

164

understands him. I wish he was home. I don't know. . . ."

"You're talking as if I'm not here. I'm *here!*" said Alan. "I don't want to be thanked, OK? I just don't want to be thanked anymore. Naomi's *my* friend, and only *she* can thank me, and she never has, because she knows she doesn't have to. And if you don't understand that, I feel sorry for you both."

With that, Alan went to his room, shut the door, and hurled his pillow against the wall, full force. Adults! What a bunch! They didn't understand anything! Naomi had more sense than Mrs. Liebman. No wonder the world was so messed up all the time.

27

Naomi was waiting in the lobby with her mother as Alan came down the stairs Monday morning. Naomi held a new leather schoolbag in her hand. Alan shook his head; she looked so awkward.

"Hey, Naomi, kid, nobody uses schoolbags," said Alan. "That's for babies. You carry your books in your arm, like this. See?"

"Uhkay," she answered. She spoke to her mother rapidly in French. Her mother seemed to be protesting, but Naomi took her books out of the schoolbag and handed the bag back.

"OK, let's hit the road, toad," said Alan.

"What is 'hit the road'?"

"I'll explain as we go."

The walk to school proved less painful than Alan had anticipated; only one boy seemed to take notice. As they were approaching the school, Jack Levine, a boy Alan had detested as a snob since first grade, whistled at them again and again. The whistle meant that Alan had a girl friend, not that Alan was a sissy. Having a girl friend, in that way, made Alan feel older. And more powerful. Alan wondered if Jack actually envied him.

"Hubba hubba," Jack said as they neared the school building.

"Go jump in the lake," Alan responded, automatically.

"What is 'hubba hubba'?" asked Naomi.

"It means . . ." Alan hesitated. "Well, it means that he thinks you're, uh, sort of, you know, pretty."

Naomi's eyes widened. "You are joking with me, *oui*?"

"No, that's what it means."

"But I'm not."

"Sure you are."

"No, I'm not!" she said with finality. But her face was reddening, and as Alan glanced at her, she suddenly looked at him and giggled.

They lined up in the schoolyard. Naomi didn't quite know what to do, but a teacher pointed to the back of the line for the 7A-R class, and told Naomi to follow the girls into the building.

Alan was glad that their English teacher, Mrs. Landley, was also their homeroom teacher. He had told Naomi all about her, including the butterfly trick.

"Now people," said Mrs. Landley, after showing Naomi her seat. "People, we have a new member of our class, a wonderful girl from France whose name is Naomi . . ." Mrs. Landley searched for her record sheets. "I may mispronounce it; tell me if I do. Whose name is Naomi Kirshenbaum, right? Now Naomi, this is 7A-R's homeroom, and after lunch, you'll be coming back here for English. I'm sure everyone will make you feel welcome,

167

and show you where everything is, including the washroom—turn around Danny Salzman; washrooms are not funny; even Shakespeare did not find washrooms funny—and . . . what was I saying? Oh, yes. *Bienvenue, Naomi.*"

Mrs. Landley beamed at Naomi as if she expected Naomi to respond in French. But Naomi sat stiffly, eyes wide, hands folded on the desk. Good grief, thought Alan. No one folded their hands like that in junior high!

Mrs. Landley walked over to Naomi's desk. "People!" she said quickly, "I want you to get your class-trip money ready, please. Twenty-five cents each. Louise, my tax collector, impound the funds, please. Check off the list as you go."

While the class was busy, Mrs. Landley gently unfolded Naomi's hands. Then she spoke softly to her, and Alan could see that Naomi immediately relaxed.

"Very well, class," said Mrs. Landley, "let's do some English."

"But it's homeroom!" one of the boys protested.

"I hate homeroom," said Mrs. Landley. "Don't you? It's a waste. Time is too precious. Now in honor of our new friend, I'd like to talk about words in English that are derived from other languages. How much of the English language do you think is truly English? Anyone? How much? Shaun Kelly?"

Shaun had been sitting sullenly, with his chin in his hands. He had glanced toward Naomi and Alan at the start of class, but after that had stared down at his desk.

"Shaun, did you hear my question?" Mrs. Landley asked.

"Uh . . . about eighty percent," said Shaun.

"Anyone else like to guess?" Mrs. Landley looked around the class. "Louise?"

"*I* don't know. I'm collecting the money."

"Oh, so you are. . . . Yes? Do you have your hand up, Naomi? How much of English is really English?"

Naomi said, in a very low voice, "I think is none, almost."

Several of the students tittered at the answer.

"Well, she's right, you know," said Mrs. Landley. "English is actually German, French . . . others, class?"

"Latin!" someone called out.

"Right."

"Greek?" a girl asked.

"Certainly. And lots more. Our language is a lovely, delicious stew. Or amalgam. What's an amalgam? Anyone?"

"A lot of stuff mixed together?"

"Yes. And the mixture makes our language strong, just as it can make metals strong. English can bend and spring back like steel. Yet it can be soft as a flower. *Une fleur.* There's your French. What other French words do we have? Would you like to tell us a few, Naomi?"

"Oh . . ." Naomi hesitated a moment. "There are so many. 'Fragile' . . . 'bouquet' . . . 'rendezvous' . . . 'occasion' . . . Is so many. Maybe because France, she conquered England in Norman Invasion. 'Invasion,' also, is French word, *n'est-ce pas?*"

"And when you think about it, so is 'Norman,' " said Mrs. Landley. "Yes, the very words 'Norman Invasion' show the wars our language has been through. I never

169

thought of that before. How nice it is to see something in a new way. Thank you, Naomi. *Merci bien.*"

Naomi looked down shyly.

Alan was proud of her. The whole class had stirred. She's woken them up, thought Alan. She'd spoken softly, but just as clearly and to the point as she had in her own apartment.

The day went beautifully. Naomi answered a difficult question correctly in math. And in French class, Alan took a special joy in seeing Mr. Florheim, an unpleasant, bullying teacher, treat Naomi very gingerly, avoiding as much as he could any conversation with her in French. Naomi had guessed it from Alan's description of Mr. Florheim and his lessons: he didn't really speak French very well at all. He was afraid of Naomi.

On the way home, Alan bought two bags of peanuts, and he and Naomi had a wonderfully silly time trying to shell the peanuts and eat them with their arms loaded down with books.

Alan saw Shaun on the next block, walking home with Tony Ferrara. Shaun turned back to see why Naomi and Alan were laughing so much, but quickly looked ahead again, when his eyes met Alan's. How about *that*, Kelly, thought Alan. I can have just as much fun with her as with you! In fact, more! How about *that*!

But if only somehow they could get to be friends again. It would be great; the three of them. It would really be great to have two friends, two *good* friends.

If only . . .

28

They did their homework together that night, on the big dining table in Alan's apartment. First, Naomi helped Alan with his French. Everything was quite different from Mr. Florheim's stiff pronunciation; the phrases blurred together in a smooth flow. When Naomi spoke French, it was musical.

They decided to do English next, leaving the math assignment till last. They had to write a brief character portrait of a friend or relative. Alan started to write about his mother, but he stopped when Naomi started giggling as she wrote.

"Hey, what's so funny?" Alan asked. "You must be writing about one of the Marx Brothers or something."

"*Non.* I write about you."

"Me! You can't do that!"

"*Pourquoi pas?* You are friend. I write about you."

"OK! Then I'm going to write about *you*!"

They wrote silently for a while. Then Naomi giggled again, and Alan looked up.

"I'm not that funny."

"You find out. Later, I read yours out loud, uhkay? Then you read mine."

"OK. But I'm not that funny."

As they continued writing, Alan grew more and more certain that Naomi was making fun of him. He suddenly erased what he'd written and started to rewrite in a rapid scrawl. He'd take care of her! Wait till she reads this, he thought. Just wait.

When they finished, Naomi took Alan's paper and studied it for a few seconds. She frowned slightly.

"I can't understand your handmanship."

"*Pen*manship."

"*Oui, oui, oui.* All right. I try. 'Naomi is twelve years old. She has black hair . . .' *Non*, my hair is brown. '. . . black hair and brown eyes and is about five foot three. She is the dumbest girl I ever met . . .' Oh, I get you! You wait! '. . . and also the silliest. She giggles when she writes, and gets the—the hiccups'? . . . *Je ne comprends pas.* What is 'hiccups'?"

"When you go iich . . . iich . . . iich—"

"Ah! *Hoquet!* In French, is *hoquet.* '. . . gets the hiccups all the time. She brushes her teeth with a hairbrush.' That's not nice. 'She blushes when someone says she's pretty . . .' I do *not*! '. . . and she is always saying things upside down because she is an upside-down cake, disguised as a girl. She would also like to . . .' Hey! I don't read *this*!"

"You have to. We promised to read each other's, right?"

"But is mean! 'She would also like to kiss all the boys

172

in the class, but she won't because she would giggle and hiccup herself to death.' You are terrible! 'So altogether, Naomi is a dumb, silly, giggly, upside-down cake, with black hair and brown eyes.' My hair is *brown*! And you are a—a cabbage!"

"That's the nicest thing you've ever said."

"Now you read mine. Here! Cabbage!"

Alan took the sheet of paper. "Uh, let's see. . . . OK. 'I met Alan Silverman in a hallway. I was afraid of him very much, because he had a stick. I am afraid of sticks. I am afraid of a lot. But I have become his friend, and now I'm not afraid anymore. In French is a word: *ami de coeur*. A good friend. A friend from the heart.' Naomi, what were you giggling at? I thought you were making fun of me—"

"Read, cabbage!"

" 'And he is a friend from the heart. If I had a brother, I would want that he should be like Alan is, because a brother should be kind, and Alan is kind.' Naomi, I—I'm sorry I—"

"Read! Read!"

" 'He is very good at flying airplanes, and school-work . . .' You're better than me! '. . . and playing baseball, and teaching songs, but this is nothing. What is something is he makes me laugh, when I am crying in myself inside. Like my father, he is. . . .' Oh, Naomi. 'And I love him. That is the end of my essay, because that is everything.' "

Naomi snatched the paper out of Alan's hand. "See, cabbage! I write nice what I feel. Not like you."

"I was only kidding. . . . I, you know. . . . I mean, Naomi, I love you, too. . . . You know?"

"Oui," said Naomi quickly, staring at the paper in her hand.

Alan felt a lightness, as if he had lifted his Piper Cub up to fly and had hurled himself into the air with it. Did she feel that lightness, too? She was so quiet.

"Naomi, you can't, you know, you can't give *that* to the teacher."

"Oh, I don't write it for Mrs. Landley. I write it for you. Here. You can keep if you like."

Alan took the paper and folded it carefully.

"I keep yours also," said Naomi, folding Alan's sheet.

"But mine's no good," Alan protested.

"I like it. It sounds how you talk sometimes. Now we have to write all over again. I think maybe I tell about the doctor I go to. She is nice person, and she is tough person. I try."

Later that night, Alan reread what Naomi had written about him, twice, before going to bed. Then, after fifteen minutes, he turned on the light at his desk, and read it again.

29

Everything went perfectly until Friday. Several of the girls at school had immediately included Naomi in their group, and she had lunch with them each day. Alan watched from a distant table in the cafeteria, and when Naomi suddenly laughed, he felt just as if he and she were laughing together. She was depending on him less each day, and it was good.

It was perfect, absolutely perfect, until Friday. But on Friday morning, Joe Condello came up behind them as they were walking to school.

"Hey! Look at that! There's *two* yids now."

Naomi turned and saw Joe's face, then quickly spun forward and walked faster. But Joe caught up.

"Hey yid!" He blocked Naomi's path. "I hear you two are married. Is that right, Silverman? I hear you dirty Jews do all kinds of dirty things." Then he spoke directly to Naomi. "That's why Hitler wants to wipe you out."

Electric and clear, without thought, without any feeling other than movement, Alan released his books and plunged at Joe Condello, crashing into his face with his fist, knocking him down. Condello grabbed Alan's legs and pulled him down, too. Everything was blurred as Alan twisted and turned, trying to get a grip on Joe. With a shock, Alan felt a fist against his mouth. His head slammed back against the pavement.

"Run, Naomi!" he called, blindly. "To school! To schoo—" Again there was a fist pounding his mouth, and blood was all over him. His face, his shirt, the street, the sky seemed to be all blood. He punched wildly, striking at Joe again and again, at Joe's face and chest and stomach.

He saw Naomi for a split second, between blows. She was calling, "*Maman* . . . Gestapo! Gestapo! The blood! *Maman!* The blood!"

"Run! Run!" Alan shouted. "Go on! Run!"

Joe was on top of Alan now, pushing Alan's bleeding face against the pavement. Joe was too heavy; Alan couldn't throw him off. He was trapped.

"NAOMI! RUN!"

Yes, she was running now. She was running toward home. Good, thought Alan. Good!

Joe hit Alan in the back of his neck. He had to get free! He had to twist free from that heavy grip. There was another blow to the back of his head, and everything went gray and fuzzy.

What was happening? Why did Joe suddenly get off him? What was going on?

Shaun.

Shaun was dancing around Joe. Shaun's wiry body, dancing.

"OK, Condello. Watch the birdie."

And Shaun struck. Quick, lightning shots, clean, sharp punches that made a crack when they landed. Alan struggled to get up. There was a tooth in the blood around him. Alan clasped his mouth. His mouth was full of blood, but there were no gaps. It was Condello's. Alan couldn't believe it; he had knocked out one of Joe Condello's teeth.

Condello was running. Shaun caught up and punched him on the side of the face, but Condello continued to race toward his friends in the distance. Shaun turned and came back.

"You stupid jerk," said Shaun. "You better get home. You're all covered with blood; it's pouring out of your mouth."

"I can't," said Alan. "My mother . . . I can't go home like this. . . ."

Shaun took off his sweater. "Here, bite on the sleeve," he said, handing the sweater to Alan. "Bite down on it. OK, look, we can go to my place; my mother's not home. Come on, you jerk. You jerky screwball, you."

As they headed toward home, Alan pressed the sweater against his face, trying to hide the blood. Shaun had collected all the books, and was struggling to keep up with Alan.

"Hey, take it easy," said Shaun. "Slow down. I've got to carry all these stinking books. All you have to do is bleed. Slow up, jerk."

They managed to reach Shaun's apartment without being seen by any of the neighbors. Alan rushed to the bathroom sink, and washed in a torrent of icy water. Cold water for blood, he vaguely remembered. Blood was still

177

coming from his mouth, but it seemed to be slowing. He examined his face in the mirror. His upper lip was puffed out, there was swelling around his left eye, and one cheek was scored with bruises from the pavement.

"Say, you look real cute," said Shaun. "Like Joe Louis just gave you a beauty treatment. You aren't going to hide *that* from your mommy, Silverman."

"She probably knows by now. 'Cause Naomi's told Mrs. Liebman, for sure, and Mrs. Liebman always tells my mother everything."

"Well, you're lucky it's Friday. I'd hate to have to go to school looking like that tomorrow. Boy, did he give you a working over."

Alan took the tooth from his pocket and waved it at Shaun.

"Yours?" asked Shaun.

Alan opened his mouth as wide as he could, to show that he had all his teeth.

"His!" Shaun called. "Wow! I never knocked out any-body's tooth in my whole life. . . ."

"That's because you're a sissy," said Alan. His mouth hurt when he spoke. He pressed a washrag against the spot that was still bleeding.

"Oh yeah? Just for that, I'm gonna knock out one of *your* teeth, Silverman."

"Sell you this one for a buck," said Alan, holding up the tooth.

"Let me see it," said Shaun. He studied the tooth, Alan noticed, with a squeamish look. Then he gave it back to Alan. "It isn't worth it."

"OK," said Alan, "seventy-five cents."

"I'd rather knock out one of yours. Your teeth are cleaner. . . . Hey, how about washing my sweater, too, Silverman. It's all covered with that phony ketchup you use when you're losing."

Shaun and his crazy insults. The insults were like a handshake, a peace pipe. They were friends again. Suddenly. Just like that. As if nothing had happened. Alan wanted to say something to Shaun to tell him he thought he was great. But how?

"Hey Shaun . . ."

"What?"

"Uh . . . Here's your sweater." Alan smacked Shaun on the head with the soaking-wet sweater.

"What was *that* for?" asked Shaun.

"That was to say, thanks for the sweater . . . and everything."

Shaun hurled the sweater back at Alan in a spray of water.

"That was to say, you're welcome. And everything."

They were friends. Alan felt a swirl of warmth, as he had when he'd come home to his own apartment after a long trip away. Everything was where he'd left it.

Alan looked in the mirror again. The bleeding had stopped, but his face was a bruised, swollen mass, and his shirt was torn and blood streaked. It was bad. What would his mother think when she saw him? And Naomi.

Naomi! He wanted to see her, to make sure she was all right. And to show her how he'd protected her; gotten bruised for her. The broken tooth for her. He'd told her she could depend on him, and now he'd proved it.

"Hey, I'm going to go upstairs," said Alan. "You going to school?"

"Who, me? I deserve a day off for my heroism," Shaun answered. "Except that I wouldn't mind seeing Condello without his tooth. Hmmm . . ."

Shaun tossed a coin, caught it, and slapped it down on the back of his hand. "I lose," he said. "I guess I'll head for school. If anybody asks, I'll tell them you were bitten by a zebra."

"Don't tell them anything," said Alan.

"Oh, don't worry; I'll think of something good. Like you fell down a sewer and your parachute didn't open."

"Thanks a lot."

"You're welcome."

Alan decided he'd better stop at his apartment first, before going up to Naomi's. He sped up the stairs, but halted in front of his door. He couldn't go in. He just couldn't. What would his mother say? Would she scream? Or faint? Or both. He'd never come home like *this* before. Alan opened the front door slowly. He could hear Mrs. Liebman talking to his mother in the kitchen. They were discussing ration stamps; the butcher was reusing ration stamps, though it was against the law. Mrs. Liebman must not have heard about the fight yet. Good. He'd rather tell them, himself. But fast, so he could go up and see Naomi. Maybe he should have gone there first.

Alan stood at the kitchen door. His mother stared at him without a word, and Mrs. Liebman's eyes followed.

"I'm home," said Alan, putting his books on the kitchen table.

"All right, Alan," his mother said. "What happened? Tell me, quick!"

This was remarkably calm for his mother. Why? Why was she calm at a time like this, but excited when he came home "flushed"? Alan could never understand her; she was at her best when he expected her to be at her worst.

"Well, Alan?" she asked, impatiently.

Alan explained the fight in a somewhat jumbled way, then held up the victory tooth.

"Disgusting," said his mother. "How can you *hold* a thing like that? . . . His parents could sue us."

"He started it!"

His mother nodded. "Well . . . you say he called you names? A dirty Jew?"

"Worse! He got what he deserved."

"*He* got? Look at your face, Alan. Look at what *you* got!"

"This'll go away. He'll never grow another tooth."

His mother looked at the tooth in his hand. Then she nodded again. "You're right," she said.

"My shirt's ripped," said Alan.

"We can get another shirt," said his mother. "Put some ice on your lip before it swells up like a balloon." She turned to Mrs. Liebman. "So what should I do? If someone called me a dirty Jew, I'd probably smack them, myself. And I mean *smack*!"

"Can I go upstairs and see Naomi?" asked Alan. "She looked pretty scared before."

"She's in school, no?" asked Mrs. Liebman.

"Didn't I tell you? She saw us fighting," said Alan. "Then she ran home. Isn't she upstairs?"

"Upstairs? Of course not," said Mrs. Liebman. "I just came down five minutes ago. She's in school."

"But she ran *home!*"

"Let me call." Mrs. Liebman went to the phone and called her apartment, speaking to Mrs. Kirshenbaum in Yiddish.

"She's not there," said Mrs. Liebman, looking alarmed. "I'm calling the school."

After the second call, Mrs. Liebman shook her head and sat down. She moaned in a low voice, *"Oy, Gott. Oy, Gott."*

"Stop with the *oy Gotts*, and let's start looking for her," said Alan's mother. "The sooner, the better. We start with the neighbors, yes?"

But where would Naomi have gone, if not home? "Gestapo!" she had called. And something about blood. He'd forgotten to tell them that.

Gestapo . . . Maybe she thought she was running away from the Gestapo. It must be that. But couldn't she tell the difference? The blood, Alan thought. It was the blood. Like with her father. It was all Condello's fault! No, not Condello's fault. Hitler's! Or maybe both. Yes. both!

He had to find her. She was alone.

30

It was Friday evening. The time for Alan's mother to light the Sabbath candles had come and gone; Naomi was still missing. In front of the Oak Terrace Arms, a police car stood in the street, its radio crackling with ghostly voices. A crowd had gathered to watch the police as they checked the roof, the basement, the neighboring buildings. On the next block, another police car was parked in front of Joe Condello's house. But the police were convinced that Joe knew nothing about Naomi; he had been in school all day.

Shaun had rushed home after school to tell Alan about his victory. Joe hadn't admitted to anyone that he'd had a tooth knocked out. He'd spoken with his lips hardly moving, a little wad of torn handkerchief stuffed in his mouth.

But Alan had scarcely listened. The victory was empty with Naomi missing. Condello wasn't worth thinking about.

Shaun had stopped in the middle of his story when he'd heard of Naomi's disappearance. "We'll find her, don't worry," he had said. But by that evening, though they kept repeating to each other that they'd find her pretty soon now, neither believed it any longer.

As it grew darker, Mrs. Kirshenbaum began to sob uncontrollably. Mrs. Liebman and Alan's mother took her upstairs to calm her. Alan's father, home from work, was walking up and down the nearby streets with Mr. Liebman, knocking on doors, asking questions, even looking under parked cars. But Alan knew it was hopeless; if someone really wanted to hide in New York, you could never find a trace. There was no use kidding themselves.

Where *would* she go? She didn't know very many places. . . . Alan thought of Holmes Airport. She knew Holmes Airport. She might have just kept on running all the way there.

"Hey Shaun, I just thought of Holmes. I went up there with her once, remember? What do you think?"

"I don't know. Could be. Tell the cop over there."

"Should I?"

"Of course, idiot!"

"OK, son, hop in the back of the car," said the policeman when he'd heard Alan's idea about the airport. "We'll take a spin up there. . . ." He called to another officer, "Hey, Danny, let's run up to Holmes. Come on."

"Can he come with me?" asked Alan nervously, pointing to Shaun.

"Yeah, sure, bring the whole block. We'll have a party."

Shaun slipped into the car next to Alan, before the policeman could say anything else.

Alan realized, as some of the neighbors stared strangely

184

at him, that they probably thought *he* was being arrested. With his swollen lip and bruised face, he certainly looked like a criminal.

The policeman at the wheel spoke over a microphone, "This is 1803. Checking a lead. Kid here says missing party knows the way up to old Holmes Airport. Going up 94th Street and taking Northern. Over."

As the police car moved slowly along, the policeman in the right front seat shone a searchlight over the darkened streets. Shaun and Alan strained to see beyond the searchlight into the blur of trees and houses. She could be anywhere!

At the airport, the car was driven over the curb, across a field of weeds, and out onto the airstrip. They drove up and down, playing the searchlight over the ground, far and near, in long thin telescopes of light. The wheels crackled in the gravel as the car dipped and nodded over the gullies. They searched for half an hour, but they found nothing.

"Hell of a thing," said the policeman named Danny. "Lucky there's no air-raid drill tonight. That'd really scare the hell out of that kid. What's she, crazy from the war, hey?" he asked Alan.

"She's not crazy," said Alan.

"Well, we got this report, says she's kind of crazy. What's she, a friend of yours?"

"Yes," said Alan.

"Of both of us," said Shaun.

"Yeah, well you know, stay away from crazy people. Let me give you some advice. Stay away from people like that. Before you know it, they'll drive you crazy, too." He picked up the microphone. "1803. Nothing at Holmes. Heading back down. Over."

Alan felt a quaver of terror in his voice, but he forced himself to say, "She's my friend . . . and if she's crazy . . . I'd rather be like her. . . ."

"Huh?" said the policeman. "I don't get it."

Than like you, Alan finished the sentence in his mind.

At the Oak Terrace Arms, the other police car was gone, and most of the crowd had dispersed. The police had filed a missing-person report; they said they could do no more that night.

Alan stood with Shaun in front of the apartment house, shivering in the night air. He saw his father coming down the block with Mr. Liebman, still hunting among parked cars and bushes with his flashlight.

"Nothing," his father said as he reached Alan. Mr. Liebman just shook his head.

The four of them stood silently in front of the building, not knowing what to do next. The street was empty now, except for them.

"Alan, the best thing for you is to get to sleep," said his father. "It's almost eleven. And your friend, he should get to bed, too."

"I'm not going in till we find her," said Alan.

"It could be all night. It could be days. Who knows where she is," said Mr. Liebman.

"The police couldn't send more than four men!" said Alan's father, angrily. "A child is missing, and they send a couple of cars for a couple of hours!"

"Listen," said Mr. Liebman. "Every policeman in the

city knows. They're on the lookout, believe me."

"No, they're not!" said Alan's father. "If she was some millionaire's daughter, or some famous actor's daughter, *then* they'd be on the lookout. But a refugee's daughter, without any money, without any pull? Forget it!"

Alan had never heard his father sound so bitter before. Yet he knew it was probably true. No one cared; she was just another missing person. Or as his father would say: just a statistic.

Suddenly, Alan's mother came rushing toward them, through the lobby. "Alan! Come with me! Alan, quick! Come!"

Alan followed his mother to the stairway that led to the basement. The heavy iron basement door was open, and Alan could see Mrs. Liebman standing in the dim light with Naomi's mother and Mr. Finch. They were looking at the huge coal pile at the side of the furnace. In front of the coal pile, like a cornered animal, Naomi sat crouched. She was covered with soot.

"Finch found her hidden under a layer of coal," Alan's mother whispered to him. "He just cleared the coal away a few minutes ago. Alan, talk to her. Say something."

Alan could see only her eyes clearly in the half darkness. Her face, caked with coal dust and grease, seemed like a mask, one of those hideous witch-doctor masks Alan had seen in the Museum of Natural History. Her eyes, alone, were there.

"Hey, Naomi, kid . . . I'm OK, now. Just a little fight we had. Nothing to be afraid about. Come on, Naomi, kid."

"Enterrez les morts . . ." Naomi hissed. *"Oui, oui,*

187

oui . . . Enterrez les morts. . . ."

It was a different voice. It was neither Naomi nor Yvette. It was ice. It was metal. Alan felt a rope of fear tightening round his chest.

"Enterrez les morts. . . ."

Mrs. Liebman whispered to Mrs. Kirshenbaum in Yiddish, and Mrs. Kirshenbaum whispered back. Then Mrs. Liebman said softly to Alan, " 'Bury the dead,' she's saying. . . . *Oy, Gott, Gott . . ."*

"Naomi, please," said Alan. "I'm Alan, remember? Naomi, I'm alive. You're alive. . . . Naomi, listen to me. I'm your friend, Alan." Please, please make it work, Alan thought.

"Enterrez les morts et fermez la porte. Oui, oui . . ."

Alan knew what that meant now. Bury the dead and shut the door. "Naomi, please . . . I want to go to school with you on Monday—" Naomi turned and leaped onto the coal pile, trying to dig in again with her hands. Her mother and Mrs. Liebman went over and, half coaxing, half forcing, led her toward the stairs beyond the basement door. As Naomi passed Alan, she whispered, as if she were transmitting a terrible secret, "Hubba, hubba . . . *enterrez les morts.* . . . Hubba, hubba . . . *enterrez les morts.* . . ."

Alan held his breath. The girl being led away, the girl whispering to herself as she stumbled up the stairs, was someone else. A mechanical girl. A broken toy.

It can't be, thought Alan. Naomi's gone. She's completely disappeared. Like a light goes out in a room.

188

31

It was a Saturday in late November. The bus seemed to stop at every corner, the bus that went from Flushing to Hollis. Alan sat with his father, silently staring out of the window. In his lap was a large paper bag.

They got off the bus in front of a stone fence with a wrought-iron gate. On a metal plaque next to the gate were the words: THE WISEMAN HOME — 1907. They walked up the path to the red-brick main building.

At the desk, a woman in a light blue dress spoke softly to Alan's father and pointed toward the spacious lawn out to the right. Then Alan's father pointed, repeating the woman's gesture. He and Alan walked back into the November sunlight.

It was warm for November. The summer had come back like a troubled ghost, wandering among the bare skeletons of trees and bushes.

A few children sat on benches, most of them looking down at the ground. There were nurses in light blue uniforms with them.

189

At a far bench sat Naomi in her green sweater. A nurse sat next to her, reading a book. Naomi was also looking down, down at her hands. As they came closer, Alan saw that her hands were moving. Her hands moved endlessly, tearing, tearing at empty air.

As he walked he felt tears coming, and he touched his father to signal that they should stop and not go near yet. To wait. To wait a moment. Alan blinked, the sunlight low in his eyes, flashing.

He swallowed several times. Then he touched his father, and they walked over to Naomi.

"Hey, Naomi, kid, look who's here."

Charlie McCarthy came out of the paper bag, and turned toward Naomi.

"Hey, where's my friend Yvette? I hear she's up in your room. Can I visit her? She's my terrific friend."

Her hands moved endlessly, and she stared only at her hands. The nurse murmured something to her, pointing at the dummy.

Alan moved Charlie closer to Naomi. "Hey, Yvette. *Je suis ici. Je m'appelle Charlie McCarthy, et je t'aime.* Hey, Yvette, come and play with me, OK?" Alan ached to hear Naomi say "Uhkay" as she had before.

But Naomi didn't look up. Her fingers tore at the air, tore the air to tiny bits, let the air fall like autumn leaves around her feet.

Alan moved so close, he could smell the scent of Naomi's sweater, of slight mint from a closet. His father moved away, and turned, because he couldn't or didn't want to watch.

"Naomi, it's me, Alan. Naomi, say something to me. Please?"

The nurse shook her head. "It's no use. She doesn't talk to anyone. I'm sorry, but it's just no use. She doesn't say a word. Not even to me. Not even to her mother."

Alan looked at Naomi once more, her hair over her face, her eyes wide and dark, her tongue out in concentration as she tore the air to shreds. He tried to seem calm in front of her, but his mind was screaming. They did it! They got her! Those Nazi bastards! They might just as well have pushed her into a truck! They might as well have killed her!

Alan let his fingers touch the edge of her sweater. Then he turned abruptly, his father following, and they walked back to the bus stop.

Alan said nothing as the bus wove in and out of traffic. His father tried to put his arm around Alan's shoulder, but Alan pulled away and stared out the window.

"Listen for a minute, Alan," his father said. "What happens in this world isn't caused by you or by me. We do everything we can, then there's no more we can do. Then, as we say, it's in God's hands. Naomi is in God's hands now. You're not God; you're Alan. And you've done all you can. But this isn't the end. Someday, you'll see I'm right. Hitler will be dead. But Naomi will be alive. And cured, and happy. She needs more time. Now, she has time. Believe me, she'll be all right. . . ."

Alan bit his lip to keep from shouting to the whole bus: *No more words! No more believe-me's! Because I* don't *believe you. They got her, and you know it!* He pressed his head hard against the window.

When they reached home, Alan told his father he wanted to go for a walk. He took his Piper Cub, *L'Oiseau jaune*, and walked slowly to Holmes Airport. At the airport, he sat down near the landing strip and watched the wind move aimlessly through the dry November weeds.

As the wind rose, Alan suddenly took the model plane and crushed it in his hands: the wings, the fuselage, the landing gear. Tore it to tiny fragments and threw the pieces into the wind. The shreds of wood and paper blew away, like brittle yellow leaves. Only the wheels were left. Alan hurled them out onto the landing strip.

"NAOMI!" he shouted. "NAOMI! . . ."

The wind blew the words back around him like a tattered scarf.

Then he threw himself down on the landing field, deep in the weeds. And he cried into the ground until the ground itself seemed to be crying, caking his lips with mud.

Temple Israel

Minneapolis, Minnesota

IN LOVING MEMORY OF
SOPHIE GOLDBERG
BY
ROSE SCHLEIFF